THE MYSTERIOUS MR. SPINES
SONG

By Jason Lethcoe
Cover illustration by Scott Altmann

Grosset & Dunlap
An Imprint of Penguin Group (USA) Inc.

GROSSET & DUNLAP

Published by the Penguin Group
Penguin Group (USA) Inc., 375 Hudson Street, New York,
New York 10014, USA
Penguin Group (Canada), 90 Eglinton Avenue East, Suite 700,
Toronto, Ontario M4P 2Y3,
Canada (a division of Pearson Penguin Canada Inc.)
Penguin Books Ltd., 80 Strand, London WC2R 0RL, England
Penguin Group Ireland, 25 St. Stephen's Green, Dublin 2, Ireland
(a division of Penguin Books Ltd.)
Penguin Group (Australia), 250 Camberwell Road, Camberwell,
Victoria 3124, Australia
(a division of Pearson Australia Group Pty. Ltd.)
Penguin Books India Pvt. Ltd., 11 Community Centre, Panchsheel Park,
New Delhi—110 017, India
Penguin Group (NZ), 67 Apollo Drive, Rosedale, North Shore 0632, New Zealand
(a division of Pearson New Zealand Ltd.)
Penguin Books (South Africa) (Pty.) Ltd., 24 Sturdee Avenue,
Rosebank, Johannesburg 2196, South Africa

Penguin Books Ltd., Registered Offices:
80 Strand, London WC2R 0RL, England

Copyright © 2009 by Jason Lethcoe. Cover illustration copyright © 2009 by
Scott Altmann. All rights reserved. Published by Grosset & Dunlap, a division of
Penguin Young Readers Group, 345 Hudson Street, New York, New York 10014.
GROSSET & DUNLAP is a trademark of Penguin Group (USA) Inc.
Printed in the U.S.A.

Library of Congress Cataloging-in-Publication Data is available.

ISBN 978-0-448-44655-4   10 9 8 7 6 5 4 3 2 1

For my dad who, unlike Mr. Spines,

has always been a very good father.

✦   ✦   ✦

I'd like to thank my wife, Nancy, for her

unending support, love, and encouragement.

I would also like to extend a special thank you

to Brooke Dworkin, who is a wonderful editor

and someone who understands the

Woodbine very well. Thank you for making

the journey with Edward and me.

AUTHOR'S NOTE

When faced with the daunting task of writing a series about the Afterlife, I needed to find some unique sources of inspiration. While doing my research, I spent a lot of time in downtown Los Angeles, finding an endless resource to mine in "The City of Angels."

"Angel's Flight," the funicular train, is currently being restored to its early grandeur, and is definitely worth visiting if one has the inclination. The car that Edward slept in while escaping from Mr. Spines in book one, *Wings*, is on the right side of the tracks.

The Bradbury Building—headquarters for the Jackal's minions and a place most certainly inhabited by Groundlings—is not far away. The building is very mysterious and was built by an architect who consulted a Ouija board before accepting the job.

But one of the primary sources of inspiration that helped me visualize what I needed to write was an unusual type of music. "Shape-singing," or "Sacred Harp" singing, has been around for a long time, but was a new and exciting discovery for me. Its strange, otherworldly music helped me shape the Woodbine and its inhabitants. If anyone would like to get a sense of what Guardian singing sounds like, I would recommend recordings like "The Golden Harp,"

"The Last Words of Copernicus," and "David's Lamentation." It was through continued listening to these songs that the world beyond ours was made visible to me.

I hope that you, dear reader, enjoy this third book in the *Mysterious Mr. Spines* trilogy. Personally, writing this series has been a source of tremendous joy and comfort. I have lost more than a few loved ones in the last five years and writing about the Woodbine provided me with an imaginary landscape in which I could see a few of them again. Al the Boatman was my friend Alan Sommerfeld. The Blue Lady was based on my own mother, Barbara. Susan the Faun makes a very small appearance and is based on my sister-in-law, Sue, and Charlie Hoof, the Groundling who owes Mr. Spines a favor, is based on my grandfather, Charles Potts.

It is my dearest wish to see them all again someday, and also to meet some of you who I won't have had the privilege or opportunity to talk to during this lifetime.

On that happy day, find me at the Dancing Faun. I'll make sure to have Jack and Tollers save a place at my table for you.

Blessings,
Jason Lethcoe
April 2009

TABLE OF CONTENTS

✦ Chapter One ✦
RECKONING

A blistering wind blew over the sea of yellow grass. Four shadows, dark against the brilliant blue horizon, slowed to a stop. Bones, the leader of the mechanical centaurs, turned his face to the wind and inhaled. There was a slight whistle as the air filled the holes where his nostrils should have been. He paused and pulled his hat lower, casting a shadow on his skeletal features.

"Macleod," he hissed. The horseman turned, maneuvering his equine body to face his comrades.

The other centaurs were no less horrifying than their leader. Blades, the biggest of the three, had the lower half of a plow horse and the upper body of a battle-scarred warrior. He was dressed in scarlet and wore a huge, pitted ax at his belt.

Blight was dressed in rags, and very thin. Her eyes blazed with an unhealthy light, and her stringy hair whipped in the breeze like a tattered flag.

Bugs, the fourth centaur, was lumpy and misshapen, his face a mass of twisted metal and rusted parts.

The centaurs were all powerful beings, but there was no mistaking who was in charge. The others obeyed Bones, for his unique power to extinguish life enabled him to end any argument and lay to permanent rest any challenger.

"How far is he from here?" Blades demanded in a flat, electronic voice.

"Two nights, maybe three," Bones replied.

"We have him now," whispered Blight.

"None escape the Four," agreed Bugs. His single, electronic eye surveyed the beautiful countryside, and his mechanical brain clicked with possibilities. Pestilence and plague followed wherever he went, and he delighted in the prospect of finding more beauty to ravage.

At a signal from Bones, the Four turned as one and set off. The pounding of their iron hooves created huge, billowing clouds of dust behind them as they thundered across the broad valley.

Edward Macleod had no idea what was coming. And even if he had, there wouldn't have been much he could do to stop them. They were the Four. And they could not be defeated.

Chapter Two
VIEW

The icy wind stung Edward's cheeks as he flew higher and higher. He was trying to reach an altitude he'd never attempted before. He glanced to his left and right, watching as his long, black wings pushed against the wind, forcing their way through the powerful currents.

He felt strong. This was a new feeling for him. Until recently he'd been nothing but a gangly, insecure fourteen-year-old with a terrible stutter. But now, as he soared above the clouds, gazing down on the green valley below, Edward felt like that part of him was long gone. It was no accident that he'd sprouted wings. He was a Guardian, a protector of mortals. And here in the Afterlife, he was at home.

Edward gazed down through the clouds at the mountain peaks. The ground below seemed miniature. If he squinted he could just make out a valley with a log cabin and a string of tepee-style huts next to it. From this height, they looked like a row of thimbles.

Edward smiled. It was Cornelius's Valley of the Blue Snails, a secret place that most residents of the Afterlife didn't believe existed. But Edward had found it with the help of his father's ring.

If only he were here and could see me now, Edward thought wistfully. His father, Melchior, would have been proud to see how accomplished at flying Edward had become. After all, his father had been an important Guardian once, before the fall that had stripped him of everything, including his wings.

It had been a tremendous sacrifice, but Edward's father had done it for Edward's mother, a mortal. He had been willing to pay any price. And pay he did, making a deal with the Jackal to join his evil army in exchange for a chance to be with Edward's mother. But Melchior had had second thoughts. He'd regretted signing the contract that required him to hand his firstborn son over to the Jackal. When the time had come for him to fulfill his end of the contract and join the army, he'd run away with his wife and newborn son, hoping to escape the Jackal's notice.

But there was no way to outrun the Corruption, a disease that turned fallen Guardians who refused to serve the Jackal into warped, twisted creatures. The disease had transformed Edward's father into a shrunken, spiny creature. Ashamed, and concerned for his family, Melchior had left Edward and his mother. But it had not been enough to protect them. A clause in the contract had led to the untimely death of Edward's mother, and the Jackal's henchmen had been after the boy ever since. Melchior should have known that trying to outsmart the Jackal was foolish, but he'd been blinded by his love for Edward's mother.

His mother. She was why, after unexpectedly sprouting wings at his boarding school in Portland, Oregon, Edward had found his way to the Afterlife. He had been told that she was there and needed his help. Now he knew that his mother was a prisoner in the Jackal's Lair, the most dangerous place in the Woodbine. And although everyone in the Woodbine told him that it would be impossible to get in, he was determined to rescue her from the Jackal's clutches.

Edward pondered his situation as he flew higher. It had grown colder, and the air was getting thin and difficult to breathe. *Just a little farther*, he thought. He wanted to see how high he could push himself.

After a few more minutes, his back began to ache and little ice crystals formed on his ebony feathers. Edward knew that he'd nearly reached the limit of his endurance and wouldn't be able to keep climbing much longer.

Preparing himself for the long glide back down to Earth, and anticipating the wonderful feeling of riding the air currents, Edward turned his gray eyes away from the infinite heavens. Gliding was much less work than forcing himself against the wind.

As his long body drew a graceful arc in the air and turned downward, Edward spotted a glittering speck on the horizon. At this distance, he couldn't tell if the figure was a bird or a Guardian.

Maybe it's Tabitha! His Guardian friend was the best flier in the Woodbine. Wouldn't she be impressed to see how high he was! Edward flapped toward the speck, eagerly anticipating the meeting.

As he drew closer, his powerful wings faltered.

Roiling black clouds punctuated by intermittent flashes of lightning filled the sky behind the other flier. Turbulence caused his wings to lose their lift. His stomach flip-flopped as he struggled to maintain his course.

The approaching figure seemed undeterred by the storm. As it grew larger, Edward could see that it was moving through the buffeting winds with greater ease than he was. He could see now that it wasn't Tabitha. Whoever it was, was a much larger and more powerful being. For a moment, Edward thought it must be Jemial, the huge Guardian warrior he'd met shortly after he'd arrived in the Woodbine.

But then a flash of lightning revealed a shiny silver object in the figure's hand. Edward gasped, realizing what it was. A chill deeper and more penetrating than the icy winds he'd been fighting filled his bones. Grasped in the powerful figure's hand was a pair of long-bladed scissors, a weapon carried by the one person Edward dreaded more than any other. It was Whiplash Scruggs, one of the Jackal's most fearsome commanders. And Edward knew with a terrible, sickening feeling exactly why he was carrying the silver shears.

Edward tried to turn back, but the wind was howling all around him and the storm was closer than ever, making any maneuver difficult. He strained, pushing himself as hard as he could against the forceful gale. The heavy wind battered his wings, slowing his progress to a painful crawl. His heart hammered in his chest. He had to get away!

He glanced back and saw, to his horror, that his bulky enemy was directly behind him. He could see the man's piggish features clearly now. Scruggs's pointed teeth were bared in an animal snarl, and his piercing blue eyes bored into Edward's own with hungry anticipation.

Suddenly Edward felt a hand close around his ankle. Then the voice he dreaded more than any other shouted in a terribly familiar Kentucky drawl, "You're mine, Bridge Builder!"

Edward thrashed, kicking his legs as hard as he could, but Scruggs held him in an iron grip. In spite of his beating wings, he felt himself being pulled slowly backward. He redoubled his efforts, but it was no use. Scruggs was too powerful!

Out of the corner of his eye, Edward saw a flash of silver. Seconds later he was falling; falling and in more pain than he'd ever been in before. A long, crimson trail of blood snaked behind him as he cascaded to Earth, black feathers fluttering all around him. His wings were gone! Scruggs had snipped them off! And Edward knew, in that horrifying instant, exactly what that meant. He was done for. A Guardian without wings was finished. Headed toward certain death!

As Edward rushed toward the Earth at a

dizzying speed, he heard a high, horrible noise echo in the air around him. At first he thought it was a howling gale, but then he recognized it for what it was.

It was the sound of his own terrified shrieks.

✦ Chapter Three ✦
ATTACK!

Edward's eyes snapped open. He shivered as he gazed around the darkened room, trying to get his bearings. Reaching a shaky hand behind his back, he felt the reassuring touch of his feathers and sighed with relief. He still had his wings!

Edward turned over, hoping to go back to sleep and forget the terrible nightmare. But he'd no sooner settled into his pillow than a bloodcurdling scream jolted him awake again. At first he wondered if he were dreaming again, but the scream was followed by a loud crash and then several panicked shouts. Edward crept over to the window, nearly falling on his way out of bed, and cautiously peeked outside.

Tattooed Guardians with green skin hurtled through the sky, diving at what, in the predawn light, looked like a group of four people riding metal horses. Edward heard more crashing sounds as the unusual Guardians' spears slammed against the horses' metal flanks.

These Guardians were unlike any that Edward had seen before—a wild bunch that Tabitha had told him lived in the mountains and forests surrounding Cornelius's Valley.

The valley is under attack! he thought. Edward threw on his clothes, the nightmare of Whiplash Scruggs still fresh in his mind. Was Scruggs behind this? Edward hadn't seen him when he'd looked out his window, but he'd learned not to underestimate his enemy. Scruggs had a way of showing up whenever Edward was least expecting him.

His pulse racing, Edward made his way out of his room and into a hallway packed with valley Guardians preparing for battle. As he edged past the throng of winged beings, he nearly collided with Bridgette, his closest friend. She seemed to have dressed quickly, and looked as frightened as he felt.

"What's going on?" he shouted, trying to

make his voice heard above the din.

"I don't know!" Bridgette shouted back. "Something broke through the Song of Warding that protects Cornelius's Valley. Tabitha's out there fighting right now. She told me that whatever is attacking us must be really powerful. Ordinary Groundlings wouldn't be able to break through such strong magic. She thinks we might be up against one or more of the Jackal's highest ranking servants."

Glancing down, Edward noticed that Bridgette was holding a bow and a small bunch of arrows.

"Where'd you get those?" he asked.

"Cornelius gave them to me last night," she said. "He also gave me something to give to you, something he said you'll need to get into the Jackal's Lair!"

Edward was about to ask what it was when the front door crashed open and he and Bridgette had to leap out of the way. Several Guardians carrying a stretcher shoved past them. Edward only got a quick look at the female Guardian with a partially severed wing lying on the stretcher before she was whisked away into a back room.

"We've got to find Tabitha!" Edward said urgently.

As he and Bridgette shouldered their way to the front door, Edward tried to quell his rising panic. Just what kind of evil beings were they up against?

The area outside the cabin was total chaos. Edward and Bridgette ducked as three low-flying Guardians carrying spears whooshed past them in the cool morning air, rocketing toward the invaders.

Edward searched desperately for any sign of Tabitha in the swarming crowd, but it was impossible to tell where she was.

"Please be okay," he murmured, thinking about the wounded Guardian he'd just seen. Tabitha was an expert flier, but whatever it was that they were fighting seemed to have an edge over the Guardians.

Spotting a nearby hill, Edward shouted for Bridgette to follow him. Maybe if they stood somewhere above the battle they would be able to find Tabitha.

He and Bridgette reached the top of the hill, huffing and puffing. Edward surveyed the battlefield, searching desperately for any sign of their friend.

Come on, Tabitha. Where are you? Suddenly, through the crowd of attacking Guardians, he glimpsed clearly whom—or what—they were fighting. Seeing the enemy up close, he suppressed a shudder.

Four horrifying, mechanical centaurs struck left and right with clockwork precision, dispatching every Guardian who stood against them. A centaur with an ax easily deflected the forest Guardian spears thrown at him, striking back at the Guardians with tremendous force. A skeletal centaur wielded his scythe as if he were harvesting wheat, shearing wings instead of grain. As each of the Guardians lost their wings, they let out terrible, heart-wrenching screams before vanishing into thin air.

A skinny, female centaur was destroying every inch of land she touched, her glowing hooves causing the ground beneath her foes to turn to swamp and suck them under.

The last centaur—a lumpy, misshapen thing with a single, glowing eye—was scattering what looked like silver seeds on the ground. The seeds swarmed over to the nearest Guardians and engulfed them. Edward watched as more than one Guardian clawed at his face and body in an effort to rid himself of the tiny, silver attackers. Whatever the little things were, they clearly caused the victim immense pain.

Edward had to do something! His stomach churned as he shoved his hand into his pocket, searching for his father's ring. Tabitha had tried to give him a crash course in ring throwing, but he wasn't very good at it yet. With a little time, he felt like he could get the hang of it, but he hadn't expected to have to use his ring so soon in a real battle!

"HROOOOOOMMMMMMBAAAAA!" Edward had just pulled the ring out of his pocket when the sound of loud, rumbling singing filled the air. He and Bridgette turned to see the Buruch, Cornelius's mammoth blue snails, gathered together at the edge of the field. They were turned toward the attackers, singing a low, booming chord that sounded like the bottom keys of a pipe organ.

The sound was so powerful that it shook the ground beneath Edward's feet, and he had a hard time keeping his balance. He knew immediately that it was a Song of Power, but it was unlike the ones that Guardians sang.

"Look!" Edward shouted, pointing at the snails. Bridgette followed his gaze. The blue snails' massive shells crackled and glowed with electric sparks in response to the magical song. Lines of fire burst outward, illuminating the shells in a bright, phosphorescent glow and casting weird, dancing shadows on everyone around them.

As the chord reached an ear-splitting volume, the mammoth blue shells sprouted enormous, deadly-looking spikes. Armed like gargantuan tanks of war, the huge creatures rushed forward to engage the centaurs. Their normally serene, almost human faces were alight with a ferocious glow. As they glided past him on the grassy field, Edward could just make out the words to the Song of Power they sang.

Azru Li, Azru Li,

Hear our song, O enemy.

To battle! To battle! Buruch, the Blessed,

Ancient snails, battle dressed.

To war we go, O enemies flee!

Azru Li, Azru Li.

The last snail had just passed when Bridgette let out a cry. "Edward, look!"

Edward glanced to where she was pointing. A winged figure was lying on the ground about forty feet away, a little apart from where the fiercest fighting was going on. Fearing the worst, he and Bridgette raced over to help the wounded Guardian.

Edward's heart sank when he saw who it was. "Oh no," he moaned. "Not Tabitha!"

✦ Chapter Four ✦
RETALIATION

Tabitha's clothes, face, and arms were bloody and ragged. Looking closer, Edward saw that she was covered with thousands of tiny teeth and claw marks.

Edward spotted one of the culprits by Tabitha's foot. It was the remains of a tiny, mechanical bug with cruel-looking pinchers— one of the seedlike things he'd seen the lumpy centaur throw.

"Oh, Edward. Look what they've done to her wings!" Bridgette said, choking back tears.

Edward hadn't noticed the absence of Tabitha's beautiful, pearly pink wings. But now he saw that the tiny attackers had stripped her wings of feathers, leaving behind two useless stumps. Flying meant everything to Tabitha. She would be devastated if she could never fly again.

Rage washed over Edward. His eyes flashed as he rose to his feet and turned to face the four horsemen. He wasn't going to let what they had done to Tabitha go unpunished.

"Edward, don't!" Bridgette cried. "You don't know what you're doing! You need more training!"

But Edward was too angry to listen. His huge wings flared out dramatically on either side of him as he raised his ring and took careful aim, concentrating with all his might.

The Four never saw the attack coming. They'd been dispatching the Guardians with ease. Even the gigantic blue snails, although formidable, were no match for them. But when Bugs reached into his pouch for more of his metal insects and found his arm severed at the wrist, they suddenly gave pause.

No enemy, mortal or immortal, had ever inflicted the slightest scratch upon them.

The Four rotated their heads and cast their glowing, electronic eyes upon their tall, thin attacker. Edward's ring returned to him like a boomerang, and he snatched it effortlessly from the air. It had been a good shot, one that would have made Tabitha proud. But as he felt the eyes of the centaurs upon him, his courage waned.

The Four possessed a weapon that went beyond ordinary steel. The Jackal had empowered them with something else—something that even their strongest enemies could not escape.

With a puff of smoke, a tiny, metal insect with a stinger no bigger than a small mosquito shot from Blight's outstretched hand. It was the smallest of the Four's weapons, but also one of the most powerful, having been enhanced by the Jackal's own magic. Its poison was a magic akin to the Corruption, but with a transforming effect that was mental instead of physical.

The metallic bug burrowed deep into the flesh of Edward's exposed neck. As it released its dark, subtle poison, a web of fear settled over him. Sudden waves of insecurity and self-doubt filled his mind. The glowing, red eyes of the centaurs focused on him, and the confidence and resolve he'd had only a few seconds earlier melted away. Voices spoke in his head, reminding him of his worst insecurities: that he was no good; that he was a skinny, tall freak who nobody liked; that he didn't stand a chance of rescuing his mother.

Suddenly Edward knew with overwhelming certainty that he was outmatched in every way. It had been a lucky shot that had injured the lumpy centaur—probably one in a million. He barely knew what he was doing as a Guardian. After all, hadn't he just learned how to fly two days ago?

Edward could not look away from the Four. It seemed to him as if the entire battlefield had fallen silent.

The horsemen continued to stare at him, watching as their invisible web snaked its way around his mind and heart.

"Edward, what's happening?" Bridgette asked, sensing the change that had come over him.

"I duh-duh-don't nuh-nuh-nuh-know," Edward stammered. With a sinking heart, he realized that the stutter that had plagued him for so long, the one he thought he'd beaten after he'd faced his fears in Specter's Hollow, had returned.

Edward felt insignificant, ridiculous, and more afraid then he'd ever been.

Suddenly Blades hefted his immense battle-ax and Bones grabbed his long scythe. There was an eerie, bloodcurdling shout as the Four galloped forward!

"Edward!" Bridgette yelled, shaking his arms. "Edward, they're coming. Do something!"

But Edward hardly moved. The voices of the horsemen echoed in his brain. *Worthless... Ridiculous... Weak... A Guardian who can't even talk, much less sing! Pathetic... just like his father...*

The horsemen thundered closer. "Fly, Edward! Use your wings! We've got to get out of here!" Bridgette shouted.

Edward couldn't think. His mind was fogged over with fear and anxiety. *It's hopeless... they're too strong... I'm no Guardian... I'm just a freak...*

The Four were very close now. Edward clearly saw the grinning metal skull of the nearest horseman laugh as he raised his deadly scythe. But he didn't care. *Better to end it now!* the horsemen's voices mocked.

Then, from somewhere deep inside him,

the words of the snails' battle song rushed into Edward's mind.

Azru Li, Azru Li, Azru Li . . . He didn't know what the words meant, but he sensed something powerful in them. It was as if the words called on a different kind of strength, one that he didn't possess, something entirely outside of himself.

He'd sung the words once before when he was trapped by Whiplash Scruggs back on Earth and needed to escape. Then, they had come unbidden to his lips, even though he was sure he'd never heard them before. This time, as he recited them in his mind, it was as if something awoke inside him. He heard a quiet voice, very different from those of the Four. It was gentle. And it radiated confidence and hope.

You don't have to listen to them, you know, the new voice said.

But they're right! They're too strong, and I'm . . . Edward thought, but the new voice interrupted him.

You are who you're meant to be, and that is enough. It is time to gather your courage and fly.

Edward didn't know who it was that spoke

to him, only that the words filled him with new purpose. Through the shadows of fear and insecurity, he realized what he needed to do. He needed to fly. The problem was, the only way he'd been able to find the confidence to fly before was by visualizing his deck of playing cards. And right now, all he could focus on were the alien faces of his attackers rushing toward him at a full gallop.

"Edward, NOW!" Bridgette screamed.

Edward calmed his mind. He tried to picture the familiar images from his precious deck, but he couldn't see them. Until he'd lost them, the cards had been like a security blanket, helping him through his most difficult times.

The Four were practically upon him, just ten yards and closing. He saw the lumpy one reach into his bag and pull out a fistful of the writhing, silver insects.

"EDWARD!" Bridgette shouted.

Suddenly the clouds lifted from his brain. The cards, every pip and every face, were clearly delineated in his mind.

King of spades with his golden shovel, jack of diamonds

with his eye patch, queen of hearts with her trapped peacock . . .

As the images rushed into focus, Edward's wings gave a powerful downward flap. He barely managed to duck the skeleton's rusty scythe as he grabbed Bridgette tightly around the waist. The big centaur's ax was raised for a killing blow, and thousands of deadly, iron-jawed insects were scuttling toward their feet.

The jaws of the nearest insect closed on empty space. Edward and Bridgette were rocketing skyward. The Four stared after their escaping prey, amazed for the second time.

There was the briefest pause as their mechanical brains whirred and clicked with this new information. Then their heads tilted back on their necks and their electronic eyes rolled back in their sockets. Their iron jaws fell open and an eerie wail filled the entire valley, an alarm that they knew their master was sure to hear.

The wail echoed off of the mountains that surrounded the tree-lined hills. But it was not just an alarm. It was also a cry of triumph. For although Edward soared among the clouds, there was a poison tether that bound him to the ground. Their poison was with him, and once infected, there was no cure. No matter how far he flew, the Bridge Builder could not escape the Four.

✦ Chapter Five ✦
TORTURE

Sometimes the Jackal's Lair resembled a dark tower with cruel spires. Other times it resembled a palace of ice. At the moment, the Jackal's Lair looked exactly like his headquarters in California: a five-story building with bricks the color of molten copper.

In Los Angeles, his headquarters was known as the Bradbury Building, and it was the most evil place on Earth. The structure was elegant, covered with iron filigree and containing dizzying flights of stairs. Most people walked by it every day, never knowing what truly went on within its secret rooms. They were oblivious to the depths of evil that lurked inside.

But in the Woodbine, everyone knew exactly what went on in the Jackal's Lair. It was a place of unnamed horror and unspeakable torture.

The Lair was hidden from view by a force field that was said to shear the wings off any Guardian who flew too close. Its borders were marked by huge, flat pieces of stone. Woodbine legend claimed that the stones were the remains of the bridges the Jackal destroyed when he fell. It was said that the Jackal drew power from the stones, that they were needed to keep his force field in place.

The legends were true.

Outside the stone wall, the landscape was dry and inhospitable. Scrub brush and stunted oak trees were the only things that grew there, and it was a place of unbearable heat.

But deep inside the Jackal's Lair, it was very cold and very dark. Groundlings swarmed through the maze of dripping tunnels and halls like a maggoty infestation. All hope was abandoned inside the Lair, for its residents functioned on a different kind of energy.

Hate. Despair. Revenge.

The very walls seemed to ooze with these feelings, filling the occupants with the traits of their lord and master, the Jackal.

It was inside one of the Lair's immense, underground caverns that Whiplash Scruggs had gathered an assembly of Groundlings to witness his moment of triumph. He'd narrowly escaped the Jackal's wrath for not capturing the boy. As far as he knew, he'd only been spared because he'd brought his master another prize.

It had been a long chase. Scruggs had tracked the boy and his father from Portland to Los Angeles and then to the Woodbine. He'd been thwarted in his pursuit several times, but finally, outside the village of Woodhaven, Scruggs had caught up with them. Unfortunately, the boy had escaped. But Scruggs was certain that Edward Macleod would return to his clutches now that he had the boy's father.

As the dank amphitheater filled with blue-eyed Groundlings, Scruggs stroked his black goatee and relished the moment that was about to come.

Melchior, known on Earth as Mr. Spines, had been captured. And every Groundling not on assignment had gathered to watch the Clipping, the ritual of severing a Guardian's wings.

Scruggs's fingers caressed the handles of his long-bladed scissors. For thousands of years, he and Melchior had been master craftsmen, creating Instruments of Power to be used with Guardian songs. But Melchior had always been just a little bit better at it, garnering the attention and praise of the highest-ranking Guardians. Where Guardians craved Melchior's unique and inventive instruments and saw them as priceless collectibles, Scruggs's were seen as well made but lacking in imagination.

Scruggs would have given much to have the success and fame that Melchior had. And it had only irritated him more that Melchior hadn't cared about the praise. He'd cared only about the work itself, something that Scruggs had never understood. What point was there in creating something if it didn't garner rewards, he thought.

It was Scruggs's bitterness over being second best that had eventually led to his fall. For him, there just wasn't enough room for both he and Melchior in the Woodbine. So he had chosen to fall. He'd abandoned his craft and turned his sharp intelligence to finding creatively cruel ways to fulfill the Jackal's orders.

And now it had paid off. He had Melchior just where he wanted him. And when he was finished with him, he would dispense with his son, Edward. Scruggs would be the most famous Groundling ever, and would gloat in his final victory.

"Who's laughing now, eh, Melchior?" Scruggs whispered to himself as he opened and shut his scissors with a deliberate *SNIP!*

Scruggs removed a silk handkerchief from his breast pocket and polished his beloved shears, admiring them with renewed appreciation. The handles were brass, but the blades were made of pure silver. He'd forged the scissors himself after much testing and trying of other metals. Ultimately, he'd proven that silver was the best for the job. It was the only metal that sliced effortlessly through a Guardian's wings.

Scruggs finished shining the deadly scissors and gazed around at the throng of hideous Groundlings. The commotion in the huge amphitheater settled down as a low-ranking

Groundling, Belthog by name, hobbled onstage and motioned for silence. The creature had a vulture's beak, a humped back, and two glowing blue pinpricks for eyes.

"Brothers and sisters," he croaked. "It is my great honor . . . *golp*"—the gnarled Groundling paused to make a disgusting, burbling sound in his throat—"to introduce to you the esteemed Moloc, known to mortals as Whiplash Scruggs. He has arranged an evening of entertainment, *golp*, that is sure to leave you both thrilled and inspired."

The Groundling introduced Scruggs with a twisted claw, and the assembled throng let out a series of thunderous squawks, grunts, and cheers. Scruggs was positively radiant at the praise, sweeping off his huge, plantation style hat and bowing low.

"So it is without further ado"—*burble, gulp*—"that I give you the most innovative and dedicated servant of the Jackal, a Groundling without equal, a genius of torture . . . MOLOC!"

More cheers. Scruggs motioned to the back of the stage and two more Groundlings, twisted apes with pig snouts, wheeled out a gurney with a small porcupine-like figure strapped down to it.

Mr. Spines was far too weak to struggle against his bonds. His face was pale and he looked half starved. He gazed sadly at row upon row of jeering Groundlings, who spat and let out a chorus of catcalls when he appeared.

Oh, this is even better than I imagined, Scruggs thought happily. Scruggs waved his hands for silence and raised his huge, silver scissors so that they caught the light of the blazing torches surrounding the stage.

"My esteemed colleagues," Scruggs drawled. "I must say, I'm overwhelmed by your outpouring of affection and obvious admiration for my person and talent."

There was scattered, halfhearted applause from the assembled Groundlings. They weren't as interested in Scruggs as they were in the entertainment to come. A few wriggled in their seats and exchanged glances, fearing a long speech.

Scruggs continued his planned speech, oblivious to his less than enthusiastic audience.

"I have waited for this moment a long time. And although our lord and master, the Jackal, can't be with us today, I received a communication from him earlier that expressed his profound gratitude to me for capturing one of his most disobedient servants."

This, of course, wasn't true. Scruggs hadn't heard anything from the Jackal since he'd brought Melchior into the Lair. But he took the fact that the Jackal hadn't eliminated him from existence for failing him again as praise enough. Besides, it felt good to inspire jealousy among his fellow Groundlings. It would only help his rise to the top of the heap.

"I promise not to keep you long."

There was more scattered applause from the Groundlings, but less than before. They all wanted him to get on with it. Everyone was eager to see the Clipping.

Sensing that he was losing his audience, Scruggs raised his voice and spoke with more animation. "But let me just add that I couldn't have done any of this without the help of one very important individual."

His eyes glinted and he gave a sharp-toothed smile. Murmurs of confusion echoed through the assembly. Everyone knew that Scruggs never acknowledged anyone other than himself. What was going on?

The fat man waited until an expectant hush descended on the crowd and then added, with a mocking bow, "I'd like to thank Melchior's son, Edward. Without his help, I wouldn't have been able to capture my sworn enemy."

The crowd cackled at Scruggs's little joke. This was the kind of thing they liked. Humiliating a victim prior to torture made for great entertainment.

Scruggs paused to give Melchior a triumphant glance.

"Yes, I must say," Scruggs chuckled, "if it hadn't been for Edward Macleod, we wouldn't be sitting here today. It was he who made a rather inept attack on one of our forces, alerting me to Melchior's presence." Scruggs left out the part about Melchior having bitten him on the arm in order to help Edward escape. He kneaded his right forearm at the memory. Melchior's teeth had gone uncomfortably deep.

Scruggs's words had their intended effect. There were more jeers from the crowd. They were eating it up! He had them in the palm of his hand. Scruggs beamed, relishing every second! Once again, he held up his plump hands and motioned for silence.

"Yes, yes, I can't take all the credit myself. Perhaps we have misjudged Edward Macleod? Perhaps he wishes to work for our esteemed master instead of following in the footsteps of his traitorous father?"

Cheers rose from the crowd again. Mr. Spines flinched at Scruggs's words, a motion that wasn't lost on Scruggs. *That struck a chord*, he mused, noticing Melchior's discomfort. Scruggs knew that his enemy couldn't bear the thought of his son signing on to serve in the Jackal's army.

Scruggs continued, enjoying the audience's enthusiastic response. "Well, I'm sure that after we catch this so called 'Bridge Builder,' and *catch him we will . . .*" he emphasized, "we will be able to persuade him that serving the Jackal is a much more rewarding venture than his current, misguided cause."

This statement was met with thunderous applause. Chants of "Jackal! Jackal! Jackal!" echoed through the mass of Groundlings; a general stamping of feet and claws, and snapping of beaks, added to the ovation. Scruggs, smiling wide, waited until the commotion had died down a bit to continue.

"So now I must ask our prisoner that all-important question, and it is one that could affect his eternal fate." Scruggs turned to Melchior and said with a booming voice, "Do you, Melchior, relinquish all alliance with the Higher Places? The Jackal himself awaits your plea for mercy. Perhaps if you show him that you are willing to return to his service and honor your contract, your pitiful existence might be spared."

Scruggs leaned in to Melchior's ear and whispered, "After I'm through with you, I'll capture your son and do the same thing to him. Two quick snips! Then I'll go after your wife . . ."

Suddenly Scruggs reared back, clutching his eye and shouting curses. Melchior's well-aimed glob of spit had found its mark.

"That was very rude, old friend," Scruggs growled, wiping his eye with his sleeve. He turned to the massed crowd and shouted, "WE HAVE OUR ANSWER. LET THE CLIPPING BEGIN!"

A roar of approval swept through the crowd as Scruggs displayed his gleaming scissors. Soon the chant was taken up again, but this time, instead of "Jackal!" the crowd was shouting "Moloc! Moloc! Moloc!"

Scruggs grinned at the use of his ancient name. Once, long ago, human empires had feared him so much that they had made sacrifices to him. He hadn't felt powerful like that in ages.

Until now . . .

The scissors flashed. A scream tore from Melchior's lips as a withered wing, a shadow of the glorious being that he had once been, fell to the floor.

✦ Chapter Six ✦
ROAD

Edward flew low, skimming over the mountaintops that surrounded Cornelius's Valley. His expression was fixed, his eyes seeing both everything and nothing at all. He was lost in his world of playing cards, an internal place that enabled him to fly.

The ace of spades, a shovel with a grinning skull. The jack of spades, in rusted armor fending off a dragon . . .

Each of the cards in his unusually illustrated deck was positioned in an elaborate, imaginary card house of his own design. Building card houses had been Edward's only true talent, and even without the aid of his real deck, he could still see exactly how everything was supposed to fit together. But where the images had once been crystal clear, now he was having a hard time visualizing them.

It took everything Edward had to hold the images firmly in his mind. Beads of sweat froze on his forehead. Edward didn't know that the Four's poison was working its way through his system, filling him with doubts and nagging insecurities that threatened to rob him of his ability to fly. The poison ate away at his concentration, making him feel like a tightrope walker who could fall several stories with the merest slip.

While Edward struggled to keep focused, Bridgette clung to the boy's thin back and shoulders as she had when he'd first flown her to Cornelius's Valley. The icy winds above the mountains cut through her pearl-buttoned coat, causing her to shiver so badly that she was barely able to maintain her grip.

Far below, she could hear the faint cry of the horsemen's alarm, a sound so piercing that it seemed to carry through the entire Woodbine.

Bridgette noticed that the frigid air was causing little ice crystals to form on Edward's ebony wings, making it harder for him to ride the currents. She was worried about him, but was afraid to talk to him for fear that he would lose his concentration. Instead, she prayed that he could focus for a few minutes more, just until they were past the mountains that surrounded Cornelius's Valley.

Bridgette's fingers were so numb that she couldn't feel them anymore. Her teeth chattered incessantly, but her eyes remained fixed on the long, silver trail far below—the Seven Bridges Road, which would eventually lead them to the Jackal's Lair.

The legends said that one day the Bridge Builder would stand at the end of that road and rebuild what had been destroyed. She knew that the countless souls trapped in the Woodbine— which had been designed only as a resting place for those with unfinished business—would be relieved to journey onward to the next of the Seven Worlds.

Bridgette's muscles ached from trying to maintain her hold. To distract herself from the pain, she recited the poem about the Seven

Worlds that her uncle, Jack the faun, had taught her.

> Earth is first, a mortal realm,
> Woodbine second, where Guardian's dwell,
> Lelakek third, for food and drink,
> Jubal fourth, a place to think,
> Baradil fifth, with secret rain,
> Akamai sixth, the Jackal's bane,
> Zeshar seventh, without the rails,
> and Iona lost when the Dark One fell.

Uncle Jack had taught her all he knew about the worlds, but his knowledge was surprisingly limited. She remembered him saying, "All we know about the worlds between the Seven Bridges is what's written on a couple of pieces of ancient parchment. And those things were copied down by Guardians who are no longer with us."

She recalled the frustration in his voice as he said it.

He'd gone on to mention that he thought there was far more to the other worlds than what was known. He believed that they had all been tainted by the Jackal's power when he fell.

All the worlds except for the Higher Places, of course, she thought. Bridgette was distracted from her thoughts when she felt Edward's long body turn and begin its descent to a grassy spot at the foot of the mountains. Her numb fingers started to prickle with new feeling as the air grew less frigid.

Edward and Bridgette rushed toward the grassy meadow. Edward landed as gently as he could, his long legs hitting the ground running. But in spite of his best efforts, having Bridgette clinging to his back upset his balance and the two tumbled into a shaggy hill of clover.

"S-sorry," Edward said, stumbling to his feet and extending a hand to Bridgette. She took it and pulled herself up next to him. After checking herself for bumps and bruises, she began to brush the grass from her ruffled skirt.

"That wasn't your best landing," she said gently, not wanting to offend him. "What's wrong? You were doing so much better the last couple of days." She smiled when she said it, but Edward blushed deep crimson.

The horsemen's poison continued its subtle work. It was fully in Edward's bloodstream now, affecting his mind and making every doubt and fear he'd ever felt much worse. He was confused and angry without really knowing why.

Scowling, he turned away from Bridgette and stared up at the majestic, snowcapped mountains he'd just flown over. *She's right. You're not a Guardian. You can barely fly! How are you ever going to defeat the Jackal?*

"Shut up!" Edward shouted, trying to quell the voices inside his head.

Bridgette glanced up, thinking he was talking to her. "I'm sorry, Edward, I didn't mean . . ." she began.

"I didn't mean you," Edward interrupted. His face was pale and he looked confused. "It's j-just that . . . ever since the b-battle, I k-keep hearing th-these voices in my head."

As soon as he said it, he knew it sounded insane. Bridgette looked at him curiously for a moment, but said nothing.

She thinks you're crazy, the voices said. *And you actually liked her! How could you ever think a beautiful girl like that would like you back? You're worthless! A freak! Telling her that you hear voices in your head? Nonsense! Pathetic!*

Edward grew so agitated his fingers began to twitch. He wanted to shove the thoughts out of his mind, but the harder he tried to fight them, the more relentless they seemed to grow.

Am I really that bad? he wondered.

You are! the voices shouted. *You're nothing! Because of you, your mother died and your father left. Because of you, Tabitha lost her wings. You'll let them all down, you'll see.*

Edward sunk to his knees, his hands clutching the sides of his head. Despair overwhelmed him. In spite of some small part of him that insisted that what the voices told him couldn't be true, it seemed much easier to believe them.

Edward shivered. Whether it was from the cold or something else, he wasn't sure. His head throbbed and he felt sick to his stomach.

Maybe I don't want to be a Guardian after all.

+ Chapter Seven +
ΠΙΕΕΤΙΝG

Jack the faun paced outside the towering
doors that led to the prestigious Guardian
Court, rehearsing what he'd come to say.

His cottage had been the first place Edward
had come when he'd arrived in the Woodbine,
and Jack had recognized the boy as the
prophesied Bridge Builder almost immediately.
But he knew that convincing the Guardians
of this would be difficult. Guardians were
notoriously slow to act, and skeptical when it
came to doing anything that broke with tradition
or daily procedure. He could only hope that
the respect the Council had shown him in the
past would count for something. He'd always
made a point to ensure that his research into the
Woodbine's vast library of historical documents
was done very carefully, and he had a good

reputation among the Guardians.

It had taken Jack just an hour to get to Estrella, the Woodbine's beautiful capital city. This was exceptionally fast, considering the fact that his cottage was over fifty miles away. But he'd had the help of two Guardians from Cornelius's Valley, who had flown him there, slung between them in a small, wicker basket. Had the circumstances been different, he would have enjoyed the experience, having never had the opportunity to study the Woodbine from the air before. But as it were, the news that the Guardians had brought him was so distressing that he'd barely noticed the journey.

He and his wife, Joyce, had been startled by the sudden appearance of two green-skinned Guardians at their home. The Guardians had told him all that had happened at Cornelius's Valley, from the arrival of the horsemen to Edward and Bridgette flying away. When he'd learned that Edward was being pursued by the Four, Jack had known immediately what had to be done. He'd left his cottage, determined to convince the Guardian High Council to act.

The stakes had been raised! He hoped that the Council would raise a Guardian army to help Edward with his quest. If they didn't act soon, all hope could be lost!

Jack had been waiting for over an hour when the majestic doors finally slid open. An important-looking Guardian emerged, her sandals making a light *clip-clopping* noise on the white marble tile as she walked.

"Jack the faun?" she asked.

"Yes," he replied, thinking that this should be obvious considering that he was the only faun in the empty corridor.

"I apologize for the wait. My name is Rachel. Guardian Zephath is ready to see you in his chambers."

Jack nodded and followed her through the entrance. A long hallway with immensely high ceilings stretched on either side of him. Tapestries depicting ancient battles between Guardians and Groundlings decorated every wall. At any other time Jack would have enjoyed the opportunity to get a closer look at them. It was rare for a mortal to be given the chance to enter the High Council's courtroom. Fortunately, Zephath was a friend and held him in high regard. Otherwise his request to be heard might have been filed in the immense stacks of waiting cases, a process that could sometimes take more than a hundred years! It was a stark reminder that time in the Afterlife was largely irrelevant.

Rachel approached a bronze door with a knocker in the shape of an eagle and knocked sharply three times. A faint voice from behind the door replied, "Enter."

Rachel opened the door for Jack and he rushed inside, eager to speak with his friend. As the assistant closed the door, Jack spotted Zephath sitting behind a huge mahogany desk that looked as if it had been carved from a single oak tree.

"Jack!" The Guardian's tanned face broke into a huge smile. He was one of the older Guardians, a handsome man with silver hair and wings. Jack approached and shook his outstretched hand.

"Thank you for seeing me on such short

notice, Zephath. I wouldn't have bothered you if it hadn't been a matter of such high importance."

"Not at all, not at all," the Guardian said, motioning for Jack to sit in one of the two elegant, leather guest chairs. As Jack sat down, he noticed that the material wasn't leather as he'd first assumed. The chair was exceptionally soft, but covered with small, red scales.

"Dragonskin," the Guardian said, reading Jack's expression. "Fought them during the Battle of Elysium Fields. They were quick, but my ring was quicker. I sure could throw back in those days . . ." The elderly Guardian trailed off, reminiscing.

Jack cleared his throat, anxious to continue. "I don't mean to be rude, but this matter I've come to see you about . . ."

"Oh, yes," the Guardian interrupted. "This matter of the . . . er . . . Bridge Builder?" Zephath shot Jack an amused glance.

"Exactly," Jack replied, feeling nervous about the way that Zephath was treating the matter. It seemed like the Guardian was making fun of him.

"Yes, yes, I heard about it from Jemial. He mentioned that there was some kind of Groundling disturbance back at your place a week or so ago. Did they steal anything important? Any of your books go missing?"

"No, no, that wasn't it at all," Jack said, trying to control his temper. "It was Moloc, and he attacked because Melchior and his son, Edward, are here in the Woodbine. Edward is . . ."

"I know, I know . . . You think he's the prophetic hero who will release the trapped souls." The Guardian waved his hand dismissively. "Would that it were true, Jack. But I'm afraid the Council doesn't have time for such matters. We've got several Guardians who need to be assigned charges on Earth, not to mention the usual backup of cases up here. We just don't have time to investigate any far-fetched 'Bridge Builder' claims. I'm sorry, old friend, but I think you've been reading too much into those old books of yours."

He offered Jack a smile and the faun felt the blood rush to his pointed ears. He hadn't expected that he wouldn't be taken seriously.

"Zephath, I think you're making a grave mistake. Edward *is* the Bridge Builder. And without the help of a troop of Guardians, he'll never succeed in defeating the Jackal. The Four have been awakened and are chasing him. Even if he gets through the Jackal's wall . . ."

"Gets through the Jackal's . . ." The Guardian laughed sharply. "You know as well as I do that that is impossible. No Guardian can penetrate the Jackal's Lair. Think about what you're saying, Jack. There's no way that the Jackal would send the Four after the boy. It just doesn't make sense."

Jack ignored the Guardian's chuckles, trying to control his anger at being dismissed so lightly.

"With faith, nothing is impossible," Jack said evenly. "I can see now that I've wasted both your time and mine. Don't bother, I'll show myself out."

Angry, Jack stood up and stalked to the richly decorated door. He ignored Zephath, who called after him, saying, "The Four? The Jackal's wall! Honestly, Jack!"

The frustrated faun opened the door and was

nearly flattened by Rachel, who had been leaning against it, eavesdropping. The young Guardian instantly straightened, turning a bright shade of crimson. Jack shot her a withering glance as he walked out of the office and made his way back down the elaborate corridor. His pulse thundered in his ears and he clenched his fists so tightly that his knuckles showed white.

"Pompous peacocks!" he muttered. "They're so caught up with their petty tasks that they have no idea what's at stake." He was just about to exit through the tall doorway that led outside when the young Guardian's voice called to him from behind.

"Is it true? Has the Bridge Builder *really* come?" Rachel said, running to catch up with him.

Jack eyed her suspiciously for a moment and then replied, "Yes, it's true."

The girl gazed at him, awestruck, and then straightened her shoulders. "I heard Jemial's report. Zephath might not believe in the Bridge Builder, but if you say it's true, I believe you. And I'd like to help, if you'll have me."

Jack gazed at the young Guardian with newfound respect. He'd underestimated the girl. He noticed the determined look in her dark eyes and smiled gently.

"Thank you for believing me, Rachel. But I'm afraid we'll need many more Guardians to help us if we want to succeed. The whole reason that I came here was to raise an army."

Rachel smiled and said, "Leave that part to me. Word of what Jemial said has spread among the younger Guardians. Give me an hour and you'll have your army."

Chapter Eight
ALARM!

Whiplash Scruggs opened the silver scissors wide, ready to snip the other wing from Melchior's back and finally put an end to the person he'd hated for so long.

Good-bye, Melchior, he thought. A wicked smile spread across his face. But as he moved the blades toward Mr. Spines's wing, a screeching voice echoed through the amphitheater.

"Groundlings to battle stations! Groundlings to battle stations! Code red!"

The Groundlings leaped to their feet and began pushing and shoving their way to the doors. Scruggs cursed his luck. There were strict rules about conducting a Clipping. The Groundlings enjoyed these events so much that the Jackal had instituted a law stating that they must always be performed in front of a large audience. The Jackal wanted his army to remain inspired, and to give his soldiers the opportunity to witness his triumphs.

Scruggs contemplated his dilemma. He wanted to end this right now. He'd waited for this moment forever! But could he disobey the Jackal?

Forget the rules! he thought. *I'll finish this without an audience.*

He placed the blades next to Melchior's remaining wing and was about to snap the scissors shut when a heavy claw grabbed his wrist.

It belonged to a tall, thin Groundling with an iron grip. The Groundling's blue eyes bore into Scruggs's own, his sharp features contorted in a mocking grin.

"And what does he think he's doing?" the Groundling said, indicating Scruggs in a rough, condescending voice. "Thinks he's too important to follow the Jackal's rules. Thinks he's too high an' mighty, don't he?"

Scruggs scowled. The Groundling's grip hurt his wrist, but he didn't want to show any sign of weakness.

"What do you want, Charlie?" he grunted.

The skinny Groundling flashed a yellow grin in response. "Well, Charlie Hoof don't want anything but the law. But he," Charlie looked deep into Scruggs's blue eyes, "he don't respect the law. 'No Clippings without a full assembly,' that's what the book says, don't it? But Scruggs thinks he knows better. And Charlie says that it wouldn't be proper. No. Negatory."

Scruggs hated Charlie's unusual way of referring to everyone as "he" or sometimes "it." The Groundling even referred to himself by his first name.

Charlie glanced down at Mr. Spines and tapped his long, yellow fingernails on his knee as he spoke. "The way Charlie sees it, this one is a bit different from the others. *Special,* if you know what Charlie means. It's to be thrown in the dungeon until we reconvene."

Scruggs wrenched his wrist out from Charlie's iron grip. Nursing it with his left hand, he glared back at the bony Groundling, wishing he could kill him on the spot. The problem was that, technically speaking, Charlie outranked him. He was head of the Jackal's police force, and when Charlie Hoof got involved, everybody had to toe the line.

"Whatever you say, Charlie," Scruggs spat.

And with that, the huge man strode from the stage, knocking over a columned pedestal as he went. Charlie stayed behind, flashing a sharp-toothed smile at Scruggs's retreat.

"He should never underestimate Charlie Hoof," he muttered softly. "Never. Negatory."

Then, grabbing the end of Melchior's gurney, the bony Groundling wheeled him from the stage and into one of the many dark passages that led to the dungeon.

✦ Chapter Nine ✦
EYES

Bridgette could swear that, for a split second, Edward's eyes had changed from their usual dark brown to pale blue. But it had happened so quickly that she couldn't be sure. She watched with a scared expression as Edward knelt on the dewy grass, his hands clutched to his temples. She approached him from behind and laid her hand on his shoulder.

"What's wrong?"

Edward couldn't explain his sudden feelings. Rage coursed through him like an angry river.

"S-stay away from m-me, Buh-Bridgette," he said coldly.

Bridgette hardly knew how to respond. She hadn't meant to insult his flying. Was that why he was so angry with her? Feeling hurt, she replied, "Edward, I'm really sorry. I didn't mean anything by what I said."

"I-I n-never said I was good at f-flying, you know. I never asked you to c-come with me."

"Edward, what's wrong? You're acting strange."

"Strange? I'll tell you what's strange." He looked at her again, and this time she was sure of it. His eyes had flashed blue! "It's strange that nothing I do is good enough. That's *strange,* isn't it? It's strange how my mother died when I needed her most. It's strange that my friends all tend to get hurt or disappear when I'm around. That's pretty strange, wouldn't you say?"

Bridgette didn't know what to do or say. She just watched as Edward stood up and paced around the damp grass, looking more and more upset.

"You say I'm strange and I say, yeah, I've been strange pretty much my whole life. I've never been good at anything. And now I'm not too great as a Guardian, either. Some Guardian," he spat. "I can't protect anybody, not even myself. Just look at me!" He flared his wings, accentuating his sticklike frame. "I'm sick of fighting it, Bridgette. I'm never gonna beat the Jackal. Never! What was I thinking?"

"I never said *you* were strange, Edward," Bridgette said quietly. "I only meant that you were acting different."

He glared at her and said nothing.

Edward turned away, and Bridgette caught a glimpse of his neck. There was an inflamed area just under his cheekbone.

"Your neck. It looks hurt," she said, moving closer.

Edward shot her a suspicious glance. "What are y-you t-talking about," he snapped.

"No, seriously," she said, pointing to the area. "It's all red. What happened?"

"Nothing happened. I'm fine . . ." Edward began, raising his hand protectively to his neck. But as he felt the area, he suddenly became aware that his skin was as cold as ice.

"Let me see it," Bridgette said softly.

Edward lowered his hand enough for Bridgette to get a peek. She could tell right away that there was something out of the ordinary about Edward's wound. The red, inflamed area was surrounded by tiny, purple veins that radiated outward in jagged streaks, like the tentacles of an octopus.

Bridgette lifted her hand to the spot on his neck, and before Edward could do anything to stop her, she did something totally unexpected.

She began to sing.

Bridgette was no Guardian, but Edward recognized the melody she was singing and knew immediately that it was a Song of Power. In fact, it was the first line in a Song of Restoration that Tabitha had sung to help his father.

As she sang, a curious change came over Edward. The voices in his head began to fade away. The fog of conflicting emotions and insecurity lifted and he felt peace settle on his heart and mind. For the moment, he felt like himself again.

"How did you do that?" he said, awestruck, as Bridgette completed the melody. Tabitha had told him that it was very rare for a human to be able to sing Guardian melodies. She'd said that mortal voices typically couldn't reproduce the complicated notes in the songs. But evidently

Bridgette was an exception.

Bridgette smiled shyly back at Edward. "I listened closely while Tabitha was singing. I can't remember the whole song, but when she sang, it sounded so beautiful. I guess I couldn't help memorizing a little of it."

As the effects of the poison ebbed, Edward suddenly felt guilty for how angry he'd been with her. He didn't even know why it had happened. Bridgette never would have said or done anything to hurt his feelings on purpose.

"I'm sorry for snapping at you," he said. "I don't know why I was acting that way."

"I think you might have been poisoned," she said. "That's a terrible wound on your neck. It almost looks like you were bitten by a huge spider!"

Edward shuddered. He hated spiders! But he couldn't remember seeing any during the battle. He raised his hand and rubbed the area. He thought back to the battle, to the centaur with the tiny, robotic insects. Was it possible that he'd been bitten by one of those metal bugs and didn't know it?

Bridgette interrupted his thoughts. "It looks a little better, but I don't know how to completely heal it. The song may help for a while, but I think that whatever was wrong with you might come back. What you need is a Guardian to sing that song, Edward. I'm only a mortal."

Edward knew she was right. And although he was technically a Guardian, he didn't know how to sing.

"Tabitha was trying to teach me how to sing Songs of Power, but I just couldn't do it. Every time I tried, it sounded terrible. I couldn't even do 'Broken Chains,' the song they teach Guardian children. It was pathetic!"

Bridgette gave him a sympathetic look. "I only know a couple verses of different songs, but we can work on it together if you want to."

Edward shrugged. "We can try, but I don't think it will do much good."

"But everybody says that you have to learn. The Bridge Builder is supposed to be able to sing. Remember the prophecy? 'His twisted tongue will utter song'? What about that?"

Edward's expression darkened. Glancing back

up at Bridgette, he said, "I don't think I'm the Bridge Builder, Bridgette. I . . . I'm not what everyone thinks I am. I'm not very good at this whole 'Guardian' thing. I can barely fly. My ring throwing is pure luck. And I can't sing."

His eyes burned. "All I want to do is rescue my mom and dad. And chances are, because I'm so lousy at being a Guardian, I'll probably die trying to do it."

Edward looked miserable. Bridgette reached over and took his long, pale fingers in her hand.

"Then just be who you are, Edward. If you really are the Bridge Builder, you'll know what to do when the time comes."

Both her words and the touch of her hand comforted him. But somewhere deep inside, he could tell that the Song of Restoration was starting to wear off. The voices, although distant, were still there, and they mocked him, saying, *When the time comes, everyone will see the truth. You're no Bridge Builder, Edward Macleod. And when you fail, everyone will finally see you for what you really are.*

+ Chapter Ten +

GROUNDLINGS

It took tremendous effort for Edward to muster up the concentration to fly again. He fought down the poisonous voices of the Four as best he could as he and Bridgette took to the air, but this time he flew much lower to the ground. He couldn't risk crashing.

The longer he flew, the more intense the heat of the sun became. Edward's long shadow was cast in sharp relief below them, following their progress along the Seven Bridges Road to the Jackal's Lair.

Most of the Woodbine was a fertile place, filled with pine trees, majestic mountains, and green fields. But as Edward neared the Jackal's fortress, he saw that the green meadows were withered. The rolling hills gave way to hard, cracked earth and baked, yellow grass. Instead of tall pines, he saw stunted, twisted trees that looked like grasping claws. And everywhere there was the faint smell of sulfur. It burned the nostrils and choked the lungs, and Edward coughed as they flew, trying desperately not to let the harsh environment destroy his fragile concentration.

They had been flying for over two hours when Bridgette suddenly shouted, "Edward, look! Over there!"

Edward glanced to where she was pointing and was so surprised that his wings faltered. He barely managed to right himself, saving them both from an uncomfortable crash on the hard-packed earth.

A horde of armored Groundlings were gathered on a stretch of dusty land not far from them. They scuttled rather than marched, like a swarm of insects intent upon some deadly mission. He could see sharp, cruel beaks and apelike faces, long taloned fingers, and pinprick eyes of glowing blue.

Spotting a grove of stunted oak trees off to the left, Edward dove toward it. He knew that if he and Bridgette could see the Groundlings from where they were, the chances were good that the Groundlings could spot them, too.

Edward landed more smoothly this time, managing to keep himself and Bridgette from tumbling to the ground. Moving quickly, he found a fallen log and pulled Bridgette toward it.

"Don't make a sound," Edward whispered as they took refuge behind the dead tree. Bridgette nodded, too scared to speak. The legion of Groundlings was headed directly toward them.

They waited, trying to keep perfectly still as the sound of the army's feet grew steadily louder. As they drew closer, a curious thing happened to Edward. The voices inside his head, which had been fairly quiet since Bridgette's song, redoubled in ferocity. It was as if the poison in his system could sense the closeness of the Jackal's servants and gained power from their presence.

Go to them! the voices screamed. *Turn yourself in! Join the Jackal's army. You are one of them!*

It was all Edward could do to stop himself from screaming. The voices were loud, and stronger than they'd ever been. He couldn't even think his own thoughts! He wanted to obey what the Four were telling him, to give himself up, anything to make them stop shouting and make the pain in his head go away. He gritted his teeth, fighting the urge to obey the commanding voices.

Suddenly he felt Bridgette's cool fingers on his neck. In spite of the danger of being overheard, he heard the girl murmuring the words to the Song of Restoration.

Through the shouts of the evil voices, Edward could make out the words to her song. They were in the Guardian language. When she'd sung them to him before, the words had been beautiful but incomprehensible. But now, for some reason, he could understand the lyrics. They didn't come to him in words, exactly, but as something like pictures that filled his mind:

Wings of light,
Renewing breeze,
Healing touch,
Gentle seas,
Falling rain in arid lands,
Health and wellness in my hands.

As she sang, the voices in his head, though still loud, became bearable. His inner fight continued, but through tremendous force of will, Edward managed to overcome the powerful urge to reveal himself to the enemy.

The closest of the Groundling troops was but ten feet from where they were hidden. Clusters of misshapen creatures limped and scuttled past them, their insect claws and booted feet thudding dully on the hard-packed dirt. The Groundlings didn't know that the person they sought was not in Cornelius's Valley, where the horsemen's alarm had summoned them, but here, right within their grasp, a hairbreadth from being discovered.

Edward watched row after row of the grotesque creatures pass and prayed that he and Bridgette would escape without notice. The army had almost completely scuttled by when, suddenly, one of the creatures in the very back of the troop, a terrible-looking Groundling with the body of a scorpion and the head of a baboon, stopped. It raised its nose to the air and *sniffed*.

Edward knew at once that it had caught their

scent. He held his breath, hoping that the evil creature wouldn't turn in their direction. It was only ten feet away, almost close enough to touch.

Stay away. Please. Just keep walking.

But the creature kept sniffing, its head bobbing to the right and left, searching for the location of what it smelled. Its icy gaze scanned the area. Then it moved in the direction of Edward and Bridgette's hiding place, making slurping sounds in the back of its gullet.

Edward ducked as low as he could, his heart beating fast. The voices, which had calmed somewhat when Bridgette sang her song, were beginning to rise again.

Go to them. Go to them. GO TO THEM! the four mechanical voices commanded.

NO!

Edward gasped as white-hot pain seared through his head.

The creature heard the noise and froze.

"Who's there?" it croaked.

Edward, fighting the blinding pain, jammed his hand into his pocket and grabbed his father's ring. He ignored the screaming, terrible voices

in his head, leaped to his feet, and shouted,
"*QADOS!*"

The ring expanded and burst into blue flame.
Without wasting a second, Edward threw it as
hard as he could at the scorpion Groundling.

"AIIIIEEE!" The Groundling's scream was
cut short as the ring of blue fire collided with its
black armor, slicing neatly through it as if it were
made of paper.

Suddenly hundreds of scuttling feet pounded
back to the area where Bridgette and Edward
were hiding.

Edward didn't have time to think about what
he was about to do. He knew that if he didn't do
something right away, he and Bridgette would be
done for!

He braced himself, mustering his courage.
The last time he'd used one of the Ten Words
of Power, it had taken every ounce of energy he
had. It was a desperate move, but the only option
he had left.

He pointed his finger at the Groundlings
and shouted in a loud, commanding voice,
"*HISTALEK!*"

There was a tremendous flash. White light exploded from Edward's fingertips and arced toward the swarm of scuttling Groundlings.

Before he could see the effect of his word, the world around him started to fade. Edward swayed on his feet, dimly aware of his enemies' screams. He fell to his knees. He had nothing left inside him. His arms trembled and the world spun. He struggled to hold on to consciousness, willing himself to stay awake. Suddenly Bridgette appeared beside him, her face swimming in and out of focus.

"Bridgette . . ."

He wanted to tell her to run, to get away from the Groundlings as quickly as possible. But whispering her name was all he could manage.

He heard her scream his name as everything around him went black.

✦ Chapter Eleven ✦
KEY

Edward awoke, not in the Jackal's prison, but inside a shallow, rocky cave. The heat from outside was diminished only slightly by the stone walls. He felt feverish and could barely move.

"Just lie still," he heard Bridgette say. "I'll get you some water."

A couple seconds later, he felt warm water trickle down his throat. He drank it and coughed. Edward opened his eyes and saw Bridgette, her pretty face dirty and scraped, kneeling over him.

"Are you okay?" he asked.

She smiled. "Just scratched up a little. It was hard work dragging you here."

"What . . . happened?" he asked feebly.

"You scared them away," Bridgette replied. "You must have knocked fifty of them off their feet when you said that word. The rest ran back to wherever they came from."

Edward paused to let this news sink in. If the Groundlings they'd encountered returned to the Jackal, news of their whereabouts would spread fast.

Edward struggled to his hands and knees. The poisonous voices in his head had diminished since he'd used the Word of Power. And although he felt feverish from the sweltering heat, he knew that they had to press on. The Groundlings were sure to return, and probably in greater numbers than before.

"Are you okay to walk?" Bridgette asked, concerned.

"Yeah, I think so," Edward replied. He leaned against the rough wall of the cave for support. "How much farther is the Jackal's Lair from here?"

"Not much farther, I think. The force field that surrounds the Jackal's Lair must be somewhere near here. But we can't risk being spotted or flying into it by accident."

Edward nodded weakly. His hand strayed to

his ebony feathers. He'd been told the stories about the Jackal's Lair being "Guardian-proof." Until now, he hadn't really thought about what they would do once they encountered the force field. If it really could shear off a Guardian's wings, they would need to find some way around or through it.

As if reading his thoughts, Bridgette said, "Remember back at Cornelius's house when I said that he had given me something to give you?"

Edward paused. In all the commotion, he'd forgotten the brief conversation they'd had during the attack by the horsemen.

"What is it?" he asked.

Bridgette reached into the pocket of her ruffled skirt and drew out a small, yellow pouch. "He told me to tell you that he made this a very long time ago, and that if you use it in a time of great need, it will always open a door for you."

Edward took the pouch. He could feel something small and hard inside it. He emptied the bag into his palm and examined the shiny, metal object that fell out.

It was a key!

Edward looked at it closely, noticing the intricate scrollwork that decorated its surface. A small mark on the handle bore the letter "F." He had no idea what the letter meant. The only thing he could think was that maybe the "F" stood for "Fallen." It seemed like a good guess since they were going to a place filled with Groundlings.

Turning to Bridgette, he asked, "Did he say where I was supposed to use it? Is there a door we're supposed to find near the force field or something?"

Bridgette shrugged. "He didn't say."

Edward pocketed the key. To Edward, the gift proved that he wasn't completely crazy to be entering the Jackal's fortress. Cornelius wouldn't have given him the key if he didn't think that Edward could find a way inside. That must have been why his father had insisted that they find Cornelius before he was captured. He must have known about the key.

Edward's mind drifted to thoughts of his mother and father. They were so physically close now that it almost hurt to think about them.

"Come on," Edward said, motioning toward the cave opening. He still felt feverish and weak, but knew that there was no time to lose. Stumbling out of the opening, he called back to Bridgette, "We'd better get going before the Jackal sends more Groundlings after us."

+ Chapter Twelve +

WALL

Edward and Bridgette trudged westward, not really sure where they were going. The sun was a relentless eye, searing everything beneath its fiery gaze. Sweat poured from Edward's forehead. He wiped it away, swatting at the biting black flies that seemed to gather wherever there was moisture. He and Bridgette barely spoke, trying to save their strength.

Edward hoped they were walking parallel to the Seven Bridges Road. They couldn't afford to walk directly on it for fear that they would be spotted by the Jackal's forces. He thought about flying, knowing that it would allow them to see how close they were to the road, but gave up on the idea almost immediately. He was too weak from using the Word of Power.

Edward's mind wandered as they walked.

For the first time in several hours, he was free to think. Although the poison was still in his system, thanks to the Word of Power the voices of the Four were distant and muffled. For the time being, he could concentrate on his own thoughts, and they were filled with questions.

Is my mom okay? Where is she imprisoned? How will I find her? What if I can't beat the Jackal?

There was so much he didn't know. He'd lived with uneasy feelings for so long that he had a hard time imagining that he could ever feel totally at peace again.

Edward glanced over at Bridgette. Her copper-colored curls were messy, and her face and clothes were covered in sweat and dust. He'd never met anyone quite like her. She was a true friend, undaunted by fear and impeccably loyal. He was glad to have her with him.

Bridgette caught his glance and smiled at him. For a brief moment, Edward forgot all about the Four. His mind flashed back to when he and Bridgette had first arrived in Cornelius's Valley. Edward had spent hours with her, getting to know her better. Together they had chatted about the gigantic snails, marveling at their beautiful blue shells. Cornelius had taught them their names, and he and Bridgette had laughed at each other's attempts to say them.

Ratablast, Gurplefart, Sneezix...

And for that brief moment in time, there had been no thought of their dangerous quest to the Jackal's Lair. All had seemed normal and filled with peace. They were just two teenagers having fun together, something that Edward had never experienced before, either on Earth or in the Afterlife.

Edward thought wistfully about how nice it had been in the cool, green valley. He desperately hoped that they might be able to spend time like that again when they completed the terrible task that lay before them.

Suddenly Bridgette stopped walking, interrupting his thoughts. The grove of twisted oak trees that had extended around them for several miles came to an abrupt end just ahead.

In the air at the edge of the forest, something shimmered. After a moment of staring at it, Edward realized what it was. His jaw fell open as his eyes traveled over an immense, semitransparent wall. Extending miles into the sky, radiating with a faint, reddish glow, was the Jackal's famous force field. It was the wall that was supposed to kill any Guardian who tried to pass through it.

Edward gulped, thinking about what would have happened if Bridgette hadn't been paying attention and they had walked right through the force field. He gave his wings a twitch, and was relieved to feel that that they were still there. The barrier was nearly transparent. Beyond the reddish glow, the barren countryside they'd been walking through continued unchanged. He could see no visible sign of the Jackal's Lair from where they stood.

"What do we do now?" he asked, speaking for the first time since they'd seen the force field. "How do we get past this thing?"

"Do you think this is where we're supposed to use Cornelius's key?" asked Bridgette.

"I don't see how," Edward replied. "The wall is almost invisible. How would we ever find a keyhole?"

Edward and Bridgette stood quietly, puzzling over the situation. After a few moments, Bridgette spoke.

"What if we check the trees?" she said.

"The trees?" Edward replied. But before he could ask her what she meant, Bridgette was striding over to the nearest oak.

The big, twisted tree was set a few feet back from the immense force field. Bridgette carefully ran her fingers over the rough bark, searching for an opening. Seeing what she was doing, and having no better ideas himself, Edward joined her. He took the key from his pocket and held it tightly, hoping that they could find a keyhole somewhere. They had looked over almost every square inch of the tree when Bridgette let out an exclamation of surprise.

"I think I found something!" She was poised by the root of the gnarled oak, pointing at a tiny hole near its base. Edward approached and saw that it did indeed look like a keyhole.

"Do you really think it could be that easy?" he said skeptically.

"What do you mean?" asked Bridgette.

Edward shrugged. "I mean, what are the chances that we are in the exact right place to use the key? We're not even on the Seven Bridges Road. How could Cornelius have known that we would come here? He didn't even give us directions."

Bridgette shrugged and said optimistically, "Well, sometimes coincidences happen."

"I don't know," he mumbled. "Seems too easy to me."

Edward knelt down next to Bridgette. He inserted the key and held his breath before giving it a turn. Deep inside, he seriously doubted that it would work.

To his immense surprise, there was a sharp *click*. Then, with a low humming sound, the faintly glowing field in front of them began to shimmer. To both of their stunned disbelief, a small hole appeared.

Bridgette smirked at Edward. "Guess you were wrong," she said, and winked at him. Then, without saying another word, she stepped through the hole in the shimmering wall and disappeared.

✦ Chapter Thirteen ✦
LAIR

Edward stared at the spot where Bridgette had been standing just moments before, stunned. He hadn't expected her to vanish like that! Was she all right? Feeling worried, he took a deep breath and followed her through the force field.

As he walked through the opening, he experienced a strange sensation. When he passed the area beneath the force field, he suddenly felt as if his entire body were on fire. Intense pain flared between his shoulders, and for a moment he thought that the key hadn't worked, that his wings had been sheared from his body.

Edward screamed. But then, just as suddenly, the pain vanished and he found himself on the other side of the invisible wall. Shaken, he glanced over his shoulder and was relieved to find that his wings were still there.

"Are you okay?" Bridgette asked, concerned.

"Yeah. I th-think so."

But even as he said it, he knew that it wasn't entirely true. Something else had happened as he'd passed through the force field. The voices of the Four had grown louder again. They seemed to draw strength from the Jackal's Lair.

Fool! the voices whispered. *You've walked right into our hands! Give yourself up! We have you now, Edward Macleod! You haven't got a chance!*

Forcing himself to ignore their cruel taunts, Edward turned his attention instead to his surroundings.

He hadn't emerged into the barren wasteland he'd expected. Instead, he was in a long, dark tunnel. Edward gazed down the immense, dripping passageway. He wrinkled his nose at the stench of mildew that assaulted his nostrils. It reminded him of his Care and Maintenance of Sewer Pipes class back at the Foundry. Images of the cruel tortures he'd experienced in that class flashed through his mind, along with the pale blue eyes of Miss Polanski, his horrible teacher. At the time, he hadn't known that she was a

Groundling sent to watch for him. But looking back, he realized the truth. Her blue eyes were exactly the same as the Groundlings he'd seen since arriving in the Woodbine.

No different, then and now, the poisonous voices inside his head shouted. *We watched you then, and we're watching you now. Come to us . . . we're waiting! You'll be one of us sooooon . . .*

"Shut up!" Edward mumbled under his breath, trying to ignore the returning headache. Then, turning to Bridgette, he growled, "My puh-parents are in here s-somewhere. Let's g-get going!"

Bridgette stared at him, taking in his pale, strained expression. "Here, let me sing the song for you again," she said, moving closer.

Edward held up his hand and tried his best to smile. It felt more like a grimace, but it was the best he could manage.

"Thanks, Bridgette, but I'm p-pretty sure it won't w-wuh-work in here. When I went through that b-barrier, something happened. We're in the J-Jackal's territory now. You're not s-strong enough."

Bridgette gazed at him thoughtfully, but didn't say anything.

Edward wasn't sure how he knew that only the strongest Guardians could use their power in this place, but all of his instincts told him that it was true. It was a place of such suffocating darkness that Bridgette's song would be squelched under the weight of it. Only a troop of full-fledged Guardians could hope to make any kind of dent in the evil he felt oozing from every wall.

Edward and Bridgette traveled down the corridor, feeling their way along the slimy stone walls as the passageway gradually sloped down. It took every bit of willpower Edward had just to put one foot in front of the other and resist the terrible voices that had risen to a scream inside his head. The voices sounded excited, overjoyed that he was heading directly to the place they wanted him to go. They continued to berate him for his weakness and his lack of Guardian skills, but there was an almost gleeful tone to the insults. With every step Edward took, he fought down a rising panic and the desire to give himself up to the Jackal.

Bridgette walked next to him, occasionally reaching out a hand to steady him when he stumbled from the incessant pain. Every time he tripped, the voices redoubled in intensity, as if his stumbling confirmed every insult that they were shouting at him. Edward knew that if it weren't for Bridgette's assistance, he would have never been able to continue.

As they walked, Edward wondered where exactly in the Jackal's fortress they had entered. There didn't seem to be anyone else around, and the passageway looked little used. Finally, after descending for what felt like an hour, the tunnel made a sharp right turn. Edward and Bridgette heard the dim sound of voices somewhere ahead of them and spotted the glow of a sickly, greenish light indicating the end of the tunnel.

They walked as quietly as they could, edging toward the voices. As they drew closer, Edward realized that the voices were arguing. He heard a loud crash and a string of curses. Then there was a small whine and a faint *pop!*—the unmistakable sound of an Oroborus bursting into flames.

When they reached the spot where the

passageway opened up, they saw a big stone room lit by glowing green torches. A rough-hewn table sat in the center, and a rusted door covered with iron rivets rested against the opposite wall. But what drew their attention the most was the sight of the two Groundlings locked in combat.

One of them—a tall, skinny Groundling with an angular face—was choking the second, an apelike thing that held a glowing Oroborus.

"Charlie don't like squealers, Rottnose! Shouldn't have done it! No! Negatory!" the thin one rasped. The other Groundling, who Edward guessed was Rottnose, gasped and squealed for air.

Edward noticed a key ring dangling from the skinny one's belt. He pointed silently at it and mouthed the word "keys" to Bridgette, who nodded in understanding. Where there were keys, there were probably jail cells. Although the voices in his head told him that he would never reach him, Edward desperately hoped to find his father alive in one of the cells.

Taking advantage of the fact that the two Groundlings were too busy fighting to notice them, Edward and Bridgette crept a little way back up the passage so that they could talk.

"I could use my ring," Edward whispered, then winced as a new blast of pain shot through his temples.

Bridgette sighed, concerned. They both sat in silence for a minute, listening to the fighting in the other room. It sounded like the skinny one had won, because other than some loud crashing noises, no other sounds came from Rottnose.

Suddenly Bridgette's face lit up. Edward watched as she unslung the bow she'd been carrying over her shoulder and took three arrows from the quiver at her belt. She'd been wearing them since they left Cornelius's Valley, but hadn't needed to use them yet.

"I've got an idea," she whispered as she strung the bow and nocked an arrow. Edward followed her back to the entrance of the big stone room.

"Are you sure you know how to use that thing?" Edward asked doubtfully. He'd never seen Bridgette use any kind of weapon.

Bridgette smiled. "I took two years of archery in my Physical Education classes back on Earth.

The coach said I was a natural."

Edward had to admit that she looked comfortable handling the bow as she raised it and pulled the string back to her cheek. The skinny Groundling had his back to them and was kneeling over the fallen body of his opponent.

Just don't miss, Edward thought. He didn't know if he could use his father's ring to defend them if she did. The voices in his head were so loud he could barely concentrate.

The bowstring gave a sharp *TWANG!* and the arrow sped away. Edward watched with a sinking feeling as it sped wide of its target. Then, to his surprise, he realized that Bridgette hadn't been aiming for the Groundling's back at all. The arrow thudded into the wall opposite them, neatly severing a thin rope that held a twisted iron chandelier suspended from the ceiling.

The Groundling named Charlie barely had time to register what was happening. With a huge *CRASH!*, a spiderlike mass of candles and twisted metal landed on him. The Groundling fell to the floor, pinned in place by the heavy chandelier.

"Great shot!" Edward shouted. Bridgette

beamed back at him. The triumphant voices of the Four faded a little in intensity, settling to a discordant murmur in the back of his head.

Edward dashed into the chamber, navigating around the unconscious body of Rottnose, and removed the ring of keys from the jailer's belt. Charlie stared up at Edward with a curious expression. Edward looked at him and was surprised to see something other than hatred on the Groundling's face. He looked to Edward as if he were contemplating something. Then he chuckled and said, "A joke it is, a very good joke. Old Jackal sends his Groundlings out, but the Bridge Builder comes in!" A raspy sound that Edward assumed was laughter escaped from the skinny Groundling.

Edward stared at him, not saying anything. After his chuckling subsided, the Groundling continued, "Scruggs would love to squeeze your skinny neck, boy, and squeeze it good. But ol' Charlie don't like Scruggs much. No. Negatory."

The Groundling's eyes flashed with hatred. "Charlie does what he likes, yes he does. Don't obey no law but his own. Not even the Jackal's!"

"Edward, we should go," Bridgette said nervously. "He's just trying to distract us, to keep us here so that we'll be discovered."

Charlie gave Bridgette a horrible smile. "Clever girl! She thinks like Charlie Hoof. But she's wrong, she is. Ol' Charlie don't want to keep you from getting to the porcupine man, no siree! Charlie Hoof is gonna help you!"

"What's this?" Edward demanded. His eyes narrowed as he studied the wiry Groundling. "Why would you want to do that?"

"Charlie has his reasons. One is, Charlie don't like Scruggs much at all. No. Negatory. And the other, well . . ." He paused, as if he wasn't sure he wanted to continue. Then he finished, saying, ". . . let's just say Charlie owes Melchior. Charlie has a few regrets, he does. Something from a long time ago, when Charlie was beautiful, yes, he was. Melchior helped him, but it was too late for poor Charlie . . ."

The Groundling drifted off, looking as if he were remembering something from long ago. Edward was about to ask what Charlie meant when suddenly there was the sound of pounding footsteps in the empty tunnel behind them. Bridgette shot him a terrified expression. It was the unmistakable shuffling footfalls of a troop of Groundlings.

"Out the door and to the left. Then left, right, left. Last door you'll find your daddy, boy. Find your daddy and tell 'im he and ol' Charlie is square. No more debt for old favors. No. Negatory."

Edward didn't know if Charlie was telling him the truth. He could easily be sending them directly to the Jackal himself. But somehow he sensed that wasn't the case.

"Thanks," Edward said, acknowledging the Groundling with a nod. Charlie didn't say anything, but offered him a horrible, sharp-toothed grin.

Edward hurried out the door after Bridgette, the rapidly approaching Groundling soldiers hot on their heels.

✦ Chapter Fourteen ✦
REUNION

The Jackal's dungeon was a sprawling maze
of corridors, each lined with what seemed like
hundreds of barred doors. Without Charlie's
directions, Edward and Bridgette would have had
no hope of finding Melchior.

Left, right, left, Edward thought, turning down
the long corridors as Charlie had directed.

After several minutes of running, he came to
the cell Charlie had mentioned. It was unlike the
other cells, which had bars for doors. This one
was covered completely by a big, iron door.

His heart trembling in his chest, Edward
fumbled through the keys, searching for one to
open the lock. On the third try, the key turned
with a satisfying *thunk* and the door swung open.
Edward's elation at finding his father gave way to
horror as he saw what he had become.

Mr. Spines hung limply from a set of rusted chains. His face was bruised and his breathing ragged. One of his shriveled, batlike wings was gone, and although he still had the other, there was no doubt that he was dying.

Edward rushed forward, shoving keys into the rusted manacles until he found one that fit. "What have they done to you?" he said, his voice choked with sobs. The manacles clicked free and Edward caught his father's small form as he fell forward. Calling to Bridgette, he indicated the rough stone bench in the corner and said, "Help me lay him down."

Bridgette grabbed Mr. Spines's feet and they carried him to the dirty bench. He lay there unmoving, his jaw hanging open, gasping for air.

Edward looked around frantically, hoping to find some water. He spotted a small jug in the corner and hoped that whatever was inside was okay to drink.

To his relief, it was filled with water. It wasn't very fresh, but it seemed okay. Edward took the water back to his father and, cradling his head in his lap, dribbled a little of it down his throat.

Mr. Spines choked down some of the water and seemed to revive a little. He turned to Edward and smiled weakly at him, revealing rows of crooked, yellow teeth.

Edward gazed down at his father, overcome with grief.

"I'll go outside and watch the door," Bridgette said quietly.

Edward didn't even hear her go. All he could think was that he was with his father. Somehow he'd found him in this horrible place. As Mr. Spines gazed up at him, even the horsemen's voices couldn't push through. Edward's eyes glassed over with unshed tears as he gazed down at his father's tortured body.

"How did you get inside?" Mr. Spines croaked.

Edward showed his father the key that Cornelius had given him.

Mr. Spines's eyes widened a little when he saw it. "The Finding Key," he whispered.

"It opened a hole in the force field," Edward said. "We f-found the keyhole in a tree."

Mr. Spines smiled at his son. After coughing

weakly, he said, "This key is a priceless treasure. It can create its own keyhole wherever a Guardian has need of one. I knew that Cornelius would help you . . ."

Mr. Spines trailed off as a coughing fit shook his entire body. After several moments, he caught his breath and let out a long, shuddering gasp. Edward could tell that his father wouldn't last much longer. His prickly face was chalky white and he could barely muster enough strength to speak.

Edward gazed down at him, wanting more than anything to tell his father how sorry he was for the way he'd treated him. When he'd first discovered who Mr. Spines was, he'd thought him horrible and ugly. He hadn't wanted to be anywhere near him. But since then, he'd realized the tremendous price his father had paid to try to protect him and his mother. Edward understood difficult decisions. After all, hadn't he left his father behind to be captured by Whiplash Scruggs? Yes, Melchior had made some terrible mistakes, but he had made them out of love, and all was forgiven now.

Mr. Spines seemed to know what Edward was thinking. He slowly raised a small, calloused hand to Edward's cheek and patted it gently.

Warm tears cascaded down Edward's cheeks. The two of them sat together for several minutes, neither one saying anything. Finally Edward broke the silence, asking the question that had burned in him ever since he'd entered the Woodbine.

"Do you know where Mom is?"

Mr. Spines motioned for Edward to help him sit up. Edward did so, propping his father up against the wall. It took several moments for Mr. Spines to find the strength to speak. The effort of moving seemed to sap what little energy he had left. Finally he found the strength to talk and rasped, "She's . . . not far . . . Jailer said she's . . . in deepest prison . . . near Jackal's throne . . ."

Edward nodded. "Ch-Charlie the jailer? H-he helped us f-find you. S-said to tell you something like, the debt he owes y-you is r-repaid."

Mr. Spines coughed for a few seconds

and then smiled weakly. "Charlie did . . . bad things . . . but all's forgiven now . . ."

"So Mom is c-close, then?" Edward's heart leaped in his chest. After all this time, all this searching, he was finally close to finding her!

But his joy was cut short. As if from nowhere, the voices of the Four reasserted themselves. Their cries rang in his ears and Edward gasped, clutching his temples.

Mr. Spines weakly gripped his son's shoulder. "What's . . . wrong, Edward?"

Edward rocked back and forth, trying to quell the searing headache and screeching voices.

Pathetic! Weak! Even if you find her, you'll never free her! You'll see, Edward Macleod. You'll see! You'll never win! She's the Jackal's now! Nothing you can do! The voices cackled with amusement.

"Stop!" Edward cried out.

"Edward!" Mr. Spines said, rallying his strength. "What's happening?"

"V-voices . . ." Edward managed. "Horsemen's voices . . ."

Mr. Spines's eyes lit up with understanding. Continuing to grip his son's shoulder as tightly as he could, he said, "Only one way to get rid of them . . . You must sing an Aria, Edward. It . . . will cure the Four's poison . . . You must sing . . . or you'll be destroyed by the voices . . ." He gasped, struggling to find the strength to continue speaking.

But Edward just shook his head, tears spilling down his cheeks. He was in agony. "D-Don't know how. I cuh-cuh-can't sing an Aria. I couldn't even s-sing the simplest S-Song of Power! Muh-muh-my voice is useless . . . c-can't suh-suh-stop stuh-stuh-stuttering . . ."

Before Mr. Spines could reply, Bridgette rushed back into the room. Her face was pale and her eyes wide with fright.

"We've got to go! They've found us!"

+ Chapter Fifteen +
PLAN

"No, no, that's wrong!" a reedy voice barked. Joyce the faun marched through her ranks of new recruits, eyeing them sharply. "You've got to sight your target before you throw. Take a moment, breathe, then fire. Don't rush it or you're sure to miss."

Jack observed the training, puffing on his pipe. He had to admit, Rachel had been as good as her word. In the past three hours, over two hundred Guardians had shown up at his little cottage. Many had immediately quit whatever they were doing to join the cause, convinced that what Jack had said about Edward was true.

Several of the Guardians were of Rachel's rank, young protectors who had recently been appointed to low-ranking positions. But many of them were eager new recruits, some barely able to sing or throw a ring. Joyce wore her gingham dress like a general's uniform and marched among them with a commanding presence. On Earth, Jack's wife had been a crack shot, and she couldn't bear to live in an Afterlife without target practice. Her reputation for marksmanship was legendary throughout the Woodbine and the new recruits listened eagerly to her advice.

Another faun, this one with blond hair and blue eyes, moved through the ranks, offering freshly made cookies and something to drink. Jack smiled. Not everyone was a warrior, but he appreciated the fact that everyone could serve in his or her own way.

"Thank you, Susan!" Jack called to the faun. She flashed him a smile.

"They're coming along nicely, but fighting Groundling soldiers will challenge them more than they realize," someone said quietly.

Jack glanced over at the young Guardian who sat next to him, her damaged wings carefully bandaged. Tabitha had been transported to the cottage shortly after Cornelius's messengers had arrived. Besides its extensive library, Jack's cottage was famous throughout the Woodbine for being a place of healing and rest.

The green-skinned Guardians had done the best they could for her injury, singing many verses of the Song of Restoration. It had eased her pain considerably, but it was still unknown whether her feathers would ever grow back. The weapons of the Four were an evil more powerful than most Guardians had ever experienced.

"They've already shown more faith and courage than their elders," Jack said. "I can hardly wait to see Whiplash Scruggs's face when he sees these brave young men and women rushing to Edward's defense."

"So you're going, then?" Tabitha asked. Jack detected a hint of worry in her voice.

"I must. I can't let Edward and Bridgette face the Jackal alone."

A long silence settled between the two of them. Tabitha gazed at the new recruits as they rehearsed Joyce's throwing instructions. At her command, they released their glowing rings. This time, many of them hit the hay bales that she'd set up as targets.

Tabitha would have given anything to have her wings back, to fly to Edward's aid. But even if she could, all the stories said that the force field surrounding the Jackal's Lair would shear the wings off of any Guardian. Even with an army, what kind of chance was there?

Jack noticed Tabitha's troubled expression. Guessing her thoughts, he said gently, "Have faith, Tabitha. It is the most powerful weapon we have."

Tabitha glanced up at the little faun in his tweed jacket and floppy hat. In spite of being a mortal, he embodied the traits that the highest ranked Guardians were supposed to possess: bravery, loyalty, and compassion.

Tabitha offered Jack a weak smile. The loss of her wings was the most difficult thing that had ever happened to her. She'd had a reputation for being the best flier in the Woodbine. It was the one thing that had made her different from the rest of the Guardians; something that had made her proud.

Perhaps too proud, she thought. After all, it had been pride that had prevented her from helping

Edward when she'd first met him. And wasn't pride the thing that had caused the Jackal's fall?

Tabitha decided that she wasn't just going to sit around and feel sorry for herself. Edward was her friend and he needed her help. Even if she couldn't fly, she was determined to do something.

Tabitha slowly rose to her feet. Surprised, Jack offered her his hand, helping her to stand.

"Are you sure you should be getting up?" he asked. "You should get more rest. There will be other battles, Tabitha."

Tabitha gazed down at him, smiling bravely. "Yes, but none as important as this one. I may not be able to fly, but I can still fight." And removing her ring from her bright blue sash, she slowly walked over to join the new recruits.

Chapter Sixteen

ENEMIES

Edward and Bridgette rushed through the dark, twisting passages beneath the dungeon, trying to throw the Groundlings off their scent. Between vicious commands from the Four, Edward's mind kept flashing back to his father's cell. They'd left him there after he'd insisted that they go on without him, that he was too weak to travel.

If he dies, it's your fault, the poisonous voices said. *You left him behind, and when they find him out of his chains they'll kill him. What a horrible son! Leaving your father when he needs you most!*

Edward's head throbbed. This time the voices were right. He *had* left his father to die.

The dank tunnel twisted left and Edward nearly slipped on a puddle of yellow slime beneath his feet. He gripped the wall for support, listening as he did so for any signs of pursuit. Straining his ears for the slightest sound, he tried to calm his rapid breathing.

"I th-think we luh-lost them," he said after listening for a full minute and not hearing anything. Bridgette stood next to him, equally flushed.

"I hope we find your mother soon," she said, gripping her sides. "I can't keep this up much longer."

Edward nodded in agreement. He wanted to tell Bridgette how much it meant to him that she was here with him. She'd followed him to the most dangerous place he could conceive of, helping him on what could still prove to be an impossible quest.

"Bridgette," he began haltingly. She glanced up at him, still trying to catch her breath.

"Yes?"

Edward hardly knew what to say. There weren't enough words to express what he was feeling. His heart beating rapidly, he leaned over and kissed her gently on her cheek. Bridgette blushed and glanced up at him.

"What was that for?" she asked.

"F-for everything," Edward replied. Bridgette blushed again and flashed him a happy, somewhat confused look. Edward, trying to prevent the moment from becoming too awkward, cleared his throat and then marched forward, saying, "We better k-keep g-going."

Edward and Bridgette continued down the passageway, each of them feeling their way through the oppressive darkness, their hearts buoyed by a new feeling of lightness. Bridgette knew that Edward liked her, and she liked him, too. She hoped that they would make it through this terrible journey and one day enjoy some happier times together.

Bridgette and Edward walked for what seemed like hours. The air around them grew warmer, becoming almost stifling as the path wound down. Sweat beaded on their foreheads. Edward was just beginning to wonder if they would ever find an opening at the end of the tunnel when the light around them began to grow brighter. Turning a corner, they saw an immense cavern in front of them. Two figures stood in front of an iron doorway. Flickering torches of green fire mounted in iron sconces on either side of the guards cast eerie shadows on their features. Edward knew immediately that they had reached the right place. Behind that door was the throne room, the place where the Jackal had imprisoned his mother.

But when Edward got a good look at the guards, his heart froze in his chest. He knew that seeing them should not come as a surprise. Of course the Jackal had chosen his fiercest henchmen to guard Edward's mother. Edward had not seen the faces of his enemies since they had attacked him outside the village of Woodhaven. Edward had barely escaped the encounter with his life.

He hoped he would be so lucky this time.

The guards seemed as surprised as he was to see him there. The two exchanged startled looks.

"Why, what have we here?" the first guard drawled in a familiar voice that Edward knew all too well. "Well, I'll be a snake's granddaddy. We have a pair of unexpected visitors, Lilith!" Henry Asmoday ran a finger across his gray handlebar moustache as he glanced over at the frail-looking woman standing next to him. The woman, her eyes covered by dark glasses, lifted her head in Edward's direction and *sniffed*.

Recognizing the scent, she bared her teeth in a sharp-toothed smile.

"Macleod's come for dinner," she whispered.

Chapter Seventeen

GUARDS

Before Edward could react, Henry and Lilith
withdrew blazing Oroboruses. Edward dived
out of the way as Henry's whistled past his head,
almost severing his ear. He heard a sharp *TWANG!*
and knew without looking that Bridgette had
loosed an arrow. Lilith, who had been injured
by a centaur's arrow while trying to catch Edward
back on Earth, heard the sound of the bowstring
and reacted immediately. She hurled her
Oroborus at the arrow and split the well-aimed
shot before it hit her face.

"You'll be our dessert after we finish with
him, dearie!" she shouted. In a flash, the
Oroborus returned to her hand and she leveled a
shot at Bridgette.

Cursing his slow reflexes, Edward jabbed a
hand in his pocket, searching for his father's

ring. But before he could withdraw it, he felt a searing pain bite into his leg. Looking down, he saw Henry's Oroborus lodged in the middle of his calf.

"Gotcha!" the Groundling shouted. The old man approached Edward, grinning wolfishly. "That's a little 'thank you' for what happened back at Echo Park," he said.

As Henry taunted Edward, Edward cautiously felt around his pocket. He had his father's ring out a second later. "*QADOS!*" he shouted.

The ring burst into blue flame and Edward threw it as hard as he could straight at Henry's head. Henry wasn't prepared for Edward's attack. He hadn't seen Edward carrying anything and had mistakenly assumed he was unarmed. The Groundling, caught completely off guard, was struck by the weapon's full force. He crashed to the floor with a sickening thud.

Lilith screamed. Edward barely noticed that he'd defeated one of the highest ranked commanders in the Jackal's army. He was too preoccupied with the pain in his leg, which felt as if it were on fire. The Groundling's Oroborus was still embedded there, scorching his skin with its red flames. He reached down and grabbed it, trying to ignore the sound of his sizzling skin. With a cry of pain, he wrenched the weapon from his leg and flung it away.

"You'll pay for this, boy!" Lilith screeched. She was poised over the body of her fallen comrade, her fists clenched with rage. Suddenly, teeth bared, she dove at Edward. She was on top of him before he could do anything, knocking him to the ground. Edward felt her nails bite deep into his left arm. He flung his other arm upward, trying to keep Lilith's razor-sharp teeth from sinking into his neck.

In spite of Lilith's small size, she was incredibly strong! Edward had knocked her back with one of the Ten Words of Power once before, but he knew that he didn't have the strength to use it again. His thin arm shook as he pushed against Lilith's throat. He wouldn't be able to hold her off much longer.

Just then, the evil Groundling's glasses fell off. Edward stared at her horribly marred face. Where her eye should have been was a gaping hole, put there by the centaur's arrow during their encounter in Echo Park. Edward could see white maggots wriggling inside the foul cavity. The Groundling's teeth snapped as she pressed down upon him, trying to get at his neck and tear him to pieces.

Edward's arm was trembling so violently, he knew that it would collapse at any second. Just as it gave out and Lilith's teeth came rushing at his throat, there was a sharp *TWANG!* and the Groundling let out a horrible yell.

Lilith groaned and collapsed, her body falling on top of Edward. Edward pushed her off. The quivering shaft of Bridgette's arrow was sticking out of the back of her skull. Edward glanced up and saw Bridgette, bow in hand, shaking violently.

Edward rose to his feet, wincing from the injury to his leg. He limped over to where Bridgette stood, but she hardly noticed him. Her eyes were locked on the spot where Lilith lay.

"Nice shot," Edward grunted.

Bridgette didn't reply. She continued to stare at the dead body, as if waiting for it to do something. Then, without warning, it happened. Henry and Lilith began to change. The human-looking skin that disguised their true Groundling forms melted away. Bridgette and Edward stared, horrified, at the disgusting apparitions that appeared in their place. Henry was a monstrous beast and Lilith something unmentionable, an abomination covered with tentacles and slime.

Seconds later, the hideous forms disappeared, leaving nothing behind. Only then did Bridgette relax and lower her bow.

They both knew that Henry and Lilith had been sent to Specter's Hollow, the place one went if they died in the Afterlife. There, they would have to face their worst fears. Edward couldn't even begin to guess what would scare monsters like Henry and Lilith, but he was sure it would be something truly horrible.

Edward shared a relieved glance with Bridgette, who looked pale and shaken. Then, with his heart pounding harder in his chest than it ever had before, he turned his attention to the big iron door.

He was finally here.

Behind this door was the one person he longed to see more than anyone else. But could it really be possible? After all that he'd gone through since he'd arrived in the Afterlife, could his mother really be this close, just behind this door?

Edward limped forward, all thoughts of his injured leg forgotten as he stretched his fingers toward the handle. Ignoring the poisonous voices of the Four, which screamed for him to stop and cursed him in voices so painfully loud that he couldn't hear anything else, he stepped forward and slowly turned the handle.

+ Chapter Eighteen +
CAGE

Nothing in the world could have prepared
Edward for what he saw next. As the door swung
open, his eyes took in the elegant, brightly
lit chamber. Directly across from him was an
empty, ornate throne sitting high on an elevated
platform. On the wall behind the throne was
a golden door surrounded by blasphemous
paintings of Guardians obeying the Jackal's
every whim. Edward tried to ignore horror
after horror as his dark brown eyes scanned
the chamber, taking in every detail. He gazed
past an endless array of severed Guardian wings
that were mounted on the walls like trophies.
Bubbling pits of sulfur steamed on either side of
the throne, filling the air with an acrid stench.
He was just about to give up, fearing that what he
sought wasn't there, when suddenly he spotted it.

A gilded cage, like something that would house an impossibly large songbird, was suspended from the ceiling in the far corner of the room. Edward's breath caught as he saw it, and he half ran, half limped to where it hung, a sob escaping from his throat.

His mother lay inside.

The world spun. Edward couldn't breathe. His mind flashed to memories that still haunted him. His mother as she lay dying in their house back in Portland, Oregon. The doctors doing nothing but taking her butterfly pulse and listening to her heart wind down. Edward had watched it all, a small boy with his world collapsing around him, wishing he could do something. He'd watched as the person he loved most left him all alone without saying good-bye.

Tears streamed down Edward's face. His vision was so blurred he could barely see her. But there she was. Her beautiful, gentle face looked just as he remembered it. She lay on the bottom of the cage, asleep, her long, beautiful blue gown spread around her like a blanket.

Edward's hand shook as he reached his

long, thin fingers through the bars and stroked the back of her hand. On her third finger she wore a golden band, a match to the ring his father had given him. It was proof that, in spite of everything that had happened, she loved Melchior still.

Edward wiped his eyes with his forearm and pressed his face against the bars.

"Mom?" he said, his voice cracking with emotion. Sarah Macleod didn't respond. Edward tried again, raising his voice a little.

"Mom, it's me. I–I've come to get you out of here."

But she still didn't move. Edward searched the bars of the cage, looking for a lock, but he couldn't find one anywhere. There was no way inside. Frustrated, he pulled at the bars, trying to separate them. He was so close! So close and he couldn't get her out!

Suddenly, from behind him, there was a terrible shriek. Edward wheeled around like he'd been shot.

Standing in the entrance to the room, filling the doorway, was the towering form of Whiplash

Scruggs. One set of his fat, powerful fingers was tangled in Bridgette's hair, holding the girl suspended in the air. The other hand clutched a pair of deadly silver shears.

Edward could only stare, fear stealing every ounce of strength from his body. "Don't hurt her," he whispered.

Edward felt a surge of desperation. In that moment, he would have done absolutely anything Scruggs told him to if he just let Bridgette go. *This can't be happening!* he thought. *First my mother and now Bridgette!*

The voices of the Four, quiet since he had found his mother, suddenly burst into peals of loud, mocking laughter, and he knew with terrible certainty that it was because the Four had him right where they wanted him.

Scruggs noticed Edward's terrified expression and smiled. Relishing the moment, he shouted, "I've finally got you, Edward Macleod, and now there's nowhere you can hide!"

+ Chapter Nineteen +
CHOICE

"Leave her alone!" Edward shouted, finding his voice at last.

Scruggs merely chuckled and held the razor-sharp edges of the scissors against Bridgette's exposed throat. "I could do that, Macleod, but I won't just yet. Not until you hear my proposal," he said in his Kentucky drawl.

Edward's fists were balled so tightly that his knuckles showed white. "What is it?" he growled.

Scruggs glanced over at the suspended cage and smiled. "I see you've found your mother. You'll find that she's in a special kind of slumber; one that can't be awoken by any power but the Jackal's."

Scruggs turned his gaze back to Edward. "Your father is also, how shall I put it . . . beyond your reach. He died in his cell a few minutes ago. So, correct me if I'm wrong, but it seems that this girl is all you have left in the world."

Scruggs pressed the blades of the scissors firmly against Bridgette's neck, causing her to whimper.

"Let her go!" Edward roared. The news that his father and mother were out of his reach filled him with despair. His hand mechanically reached into his pocket, searching for his father's ring. He wouldn't let the Jackal steal any more of his loved ones. He already had Edward's parents. He couldn't have Bridgette, too!

"None of that, Macleod!" Scruggs hissed, jerking hard on Bridgette's hair. Tears flowed down the girl's cheeks, but Edward could tell that she was doing everything she could not to let Scruggs see her weaken.

Edward removed his hand from his pocket. He'd never felt so helpless. "Just tell me what you want!"

"To your left, you'll see a large, stone table. Upon it is a contract that states that you'll give yourself to the Jackal's service."

Edward looked over and saw the ornate table with the roll of parchment on it.

Scruggs continued, "The Jackal has big plans for you, Macleod. He's decided to make you a captain. You'll have legions of Groundlings under your command. All you have to do is sign your name to that piece of paper and it's done."

Edward glanced up sharply. Scruggs wore an expression of greedy anticipation on his face. Edward didn't know what to do. If he didn't sign the paper, Scruggs might kill Bridgette.

"You have no choice, Edward. Sign the paper," Scruggs said.

Bridgette saw Edward's hesitation and shouted, "Don't do it, Edward!" But she was quickly silenced by Scruggs's hard jerk on the back of her head.

"And if I do this, I have your word that you won't hurt her?" Edward demanded.

"Of course," Scruggs replied.

The voices of the Four were exultant. Edward knew that he couldn't trust Whiplash Scruggs, but he had no choice.

As if in a dream, he felt himself walk over to

the table and pick up the long black plume. He recognized it immediately.

It was one of his own feathers.

Feeling sick to his stomach, Edward picked up the pen. Bridgette writhed in Whiplash Scruggs's grip and shouted desperately for Edward to stop. But Edward was cornered. He couldn't stand to lose anyone else he cared about. His mother was under a spell that he had no hope of breaking. His father was dead. This was his only option; a last, desperate move to save Bridgette.

Looking down at the ancient contract, he saw the names of other Guardians who had signed it before him. Row upon countless row of doomed Guardian signatures decorated the contract, each one dated at the time of their "Fall." He scanned the long list, wondering what had brought each of the Guardians to the terrible choice to join the Jackal's army.

Just then his eyes fell on a signature near the end of the list. The hair on his arms and scalp stood on end as he realized that he was looking at the very same contract that had shaped his life so long ago. He read the ornate signature several times, hardly believing what he was seeing.

Melchior.

It was his father's name. And there was a
blank space just below it, an area that seemed as
if it had been purposely left that way. Had the
Jackal always known that someday Edward would
add his name to the very same contract that had
doomed his father?

With a sinking feeling, Edward realized the
truth. For all his thinking that he could somehow
become the legendary hero who would defeat the
Jackal, in the end, fate had decided his destiny
for him. He didn't have a choice.

Edward's eyes slowly began to change, growing
paler as he dipped the quill in an ebony bottle
filled with crimson ink. The poisonous voices of
the Four gibbered wildly, shouting in triumph.

He's one of us! He's one of us! He's one of us!

And for the first time, Edward didn't resist
their taunts. As he placed the tip of the quill
against the parchment, he realized for the first
time that the Four weren't just taunting him,
making his worst fears seem real.

This time what they were saying was true.

✦ Chapter Twenty ✦
GIFT

Scruggs watched as Edward added his name to the long list of fallen Guardians. He shoved the girl away, fulfilling his end of the bargain. He would deal with her later. Right now there was only one thought in his mind.

Edward is the Jackal's servant!

He'd finally done it! After all the failed attempts, Scruggs had finally fulfilled his mission. He had turned Edward to the Jackal's side. His master would be pleased! The relief he felt was incredible. He glanced across the room at the golden door, the one that led to the Jackal's inner sanctum. He knew that his horrifying master was in there at this very moment, aware of all that was happening. Scruggs pictured the single yellow eye, the only part of the Jackal that wasn't a machine, rolling with pleasure. Edward Macleod was no longer a threat. There would be no Bridge Builder. And the Jackal would emerge the victor in his age-old war against the Higher Places.

Scruggs was so entranced by his wonderful vision that he never heard the crumpled form sneak up behind him. The figure pulled an iron torch from the wall and threw it toward Scruggs. It flew through the air, colliding with Scruggs's precious shears and sending them to the ground in a shower of sparks. Years of throwing rings had given the attacker incredible accuracy.

A voice Scruggs knew too well, one that he had thought was gone forever, rang out from behind him.

"It's not over, Edward! You still have a choice!"

Edward glanced up sharply. He didn't recognize the man calling to him. Edward's eyes had turned pale blue and he could see nothing but shadows and death. The Four celebrated wildly in his head, telling him that he'd finally fulfilled his destiny. But Edward barely heard them now. Something deep inside made him pause. What the little man had said confused him. He stared at him, watching as he approached Whiplash Scruggs with a determined look on his face . . .

The man gathered his strength. His body tensed, anticipating what he was about to do. He knew it would be the last great act he would ever accomplish.

He gave Edward a last look. And as Edward stared back at him, the clouds of confusion disappeared and a look of dawning realization came over his face.

Contentment flooded Mr. Spines. He knew beyond a doubt that his son would be okay. He turned back to Whiplash Scruggs and, gathering all of his strength, shouted one of the Ten ancient Words of Power.

"HISTALEK!"

There was a hissing sound, like someone turning on a gas valve. Then, with a loud *CRACK!*, bolts of brilliant blue lightning arced from Mr. Spines's outstretched fingers, slamming into Whiplash Scruggs with tremendous force.

The huge man barely had time to register

what was happening before he was lifted off the ground and sent flying. He slammed into the far wall of the Jackal's chamber with a tremendous crash.

The tiny body of Mr. Spines hit the marble floor with a lifeless thud. As he sank to the ground, the force of the words he'd left with Edward hit home. Edward realized that his father had given him one last gift.

He understood his father now more than he ever had. Once, long ago, his father had signed the contract with the Jackal for a chance to be with Edward's mother. But when Mr. Spines had realized what he'd done, that it was the wrong way to get what he wanted, he'd *chosen* to break the contract.

Edward stared down at the contract. His name was printed in scarlet ink just below his father's. But now he saw it for what it truly was.

It was just a piece of paper. Even now, he still had a choice.

It wasn't over.

The words of the poem his father had recited to him so long ago came back:

There are seven bridges between the worlds
And five of them are broken.
The sixth one has no rails to hold
And the seventh one was stolen.
Captive then, the wand'ring dead,
For an epoch the world's turn.
When halfway from the mortal realm,
A builder will return.
His twisted tongue will utter song,
The champion will arise,
But fallen Groundling or gentle Guard,
His choices will decide.

He always had a choice.

And remembering that made all the difference to Edward Macleod.

✦ ✦ ✦

Whiplash Scruggs regained his footing just in time to hear the sound of something being ripped in half. Looking up, the immense Groundling saw Edward standing tall, one half of the ancient contract held in each of his hands.

The boy turned to look at Scruggs. All traces of blue were gone from his eyes.

Whiplash Scruggs stood, still smoking from where the lightning had struck. Melchior's Word of Power had melted his mortal disguise. No longer did he look like a massive Kentucky plantation owner sporting a black goatee. Instead, what stood in Scruggs's place was the being he truly was.

Beneath the layers of human costume was the blackened head of a bull. Where his eyes should have been were burning coals. His arms and chest were human, but his legs and feet were serpent's coils. Cruel, twisted horns protruded from his blasphemous head. A crumpled, useless pair of leathery wings sat on his massive back, the only indication that he'd once been a Guardian.

The Groundling howled, a bellow filled with hate for all those who didn't serve his cruel master, the Jackal. Then, with a roar, he slithered forward, his powerful hands extended toward Edward like bared claws. His eyes blazed with hatred, every fiber of his being intent on destroying the boy once and for all.

Edward stood his ground against the hideous beast. All fear was wiped from his mind. The voices of the Four still raged, but their words had no effect on him. No matter what they said he was, he knew that he could be whatever he chose to be.

And he chose to be a Guardian.

✦ Chapter Twenty-One ✦
SONG

When the horrible thing that had been Whiplash Scruggs was just ten feet away, Edward did something that he had never done before. He began to sing.

The melody started slowly, something light and nearly tuneless. But as he continued, not giving in to the insecurity that had always stopped him before, the melody took on a power all its own. The song grew, and it was a new song, one that he'd never been taught. He sang the words as they came into his mind and it became his own Song of Power.

As Scruggs leaped for Edward, bright chains appeared, woven from Edward's melody, and bound him in place. The creature howled in frustration as he was lifted into the air, helpless.

The walls of the Jackal's throne room began

to shake. Edward continued to sing, a fierce joy radiating from the depths of his soul. Bridgette watched, stunned, as the ring from his mother's hand slid from her finger and rose into the air. It pulsed with a soft, golden glow as it floated toward Edward. His father's ring rose from Edward's palm to meet it. As the song continued, the rings grew in size, becoming twin halos of blue fire that settled above Edward's head.

The song took on new power and strength. Edward's ebony wings stretched out on either side of him and he rose into the air like a majestic bird. His face shone with a joy so bright that it cast shadows on the room, making everything the Jackal possessed look worn and tattered.

Swarms of Groundlings, alerted by the rumbling in the Jackal's chamber, rushed into the room with weapons drawn. But when they saw Edward, they faltered, not knowing what to do.

Their blue eyes grew wide as they saw Scruggs, writhing and bellowing in his glowing chains. They stared, stunned, as pieces of the walls chipped and fell to the marble floor. Doom had come upon them, and for the first time since they fell, a new fear reigned in their hearts. One that suggested that they might not prevail after all.

Chapter Twenty-Two

ARMY

Jack and his army of young Guardians camped in front of the glowing force field at the border of the Jackal's fortress. They had arrived forty-five minutes earlier, but had been stopped by the nearly transparent barrier that threatened to destroy their wings, or worse.

And so they waited, not knowing what would happen, but having faith that something would.

And something did.

The force of Edward's Song of Power radiated outward, dissolving the barrier that surrounded the fortress. The army stood, dumbfounded, as the terrifying wall melted away and revealed the Jackal's Lair standing before them, unguarded.

There was a tremendous shout, and then, with a mighty flap of wings, the troop of young Guardians took to the air.

✦ ✦ ✦

The miles of earth that were above Edward
gave way to the powerful melody. With a
tremendous *CRACK!*, the ground spilt open,
sending rays of sunlight into the shadowy depths
of the Jackal's Lair. The assembled Groundlings
hid their eyes as the piercing sunlight split the
darkness. Guardians poured through the crack,
singing at the top of their lungs, their rings
ablaze with blue fire.

The sight of their hated foes urged the
Groundling forces on. As one, the assembled
throng shouted "*NSH!*" and raised their flaming
Oroboruses, ready to fight for their lives.

Seconds later, the room was filled with deadly
arcs of blue and red fire. A thunderous *BOOM!*
rocked the cavern as the enemy forces collided,
shaking the Jackal's fortress to its core.

Edward knew what he had to do. Leaving
the Guardians to deal with the hordes of
terrified Groundlings, he moved to the golden
door behind the Jackal's throne. It was time
to confront the being behind it all, the one

responsible for all the pain Edward and the residents of the Woodbine had endured.

The door gave way at his touch and, still singing, he entered the forbidden chamber.

✦ ✦ ✦

The chamber was dark, making it difficult for Edward to see. He felt his way forward, resting his hand against a nearby wall. The moment his fingers brushed it, he recoiled. The surface was warm, pulsing with what felt like a living heartbeat!

As his eyes grew accustomed to the darkness, he saw that, instead of stone, the chamber seemed to be made of living tissue. It quivered, sending some kind of power to the twisted thing that crouched in the center of the room.

Whatever Edward had imagined the Jackal to look like, it wasn't this. He had expected something like Whiplash Scruggs or Henry and Lilith.

This was something else. An abomination.

What he saw reminded him of the machines the students at the Foundry had been forced to repair. Rusted gauges released pressurized steam. Gears spun and driveshafts turned.

There was the sound of a bellows inflating, and a reedy laugh, like the cackle of a wild dog, filled the air. In the center of the machine, a lidless orb swiveled around and focused on him. As it did, Edward knew with certainty that the eye, the only part of the Jackal that wasn't made of machinery, recognized him.

Edward gazed in horror at this, the Jackal's remains, suddenly aware that his lips were moving but no sound was coming out. From somewhere in the darkness he heard the whine of a turbine engine powering up. Deep inside, he felt certain that the Jackal was about to unleash every bit of evil power he had to defend himself. He had no idea what form it would take or what kind of torture the Jackal would inflict upon him. All he knew was that if he didn't do something quickly, it would all be over.

Edward lifted his voice without hesitation, trusting that whatever song came to his lips would be the right one. He halfway intended to repeat what he'd sung in the chamber outside.

But at the last moment, something inside of him decided differently. A brand-new melody came unbidden to his lips.

To his surprise, what emerged was an Aria, the highest form of Guardian song. It was a rare and wonderful kind of music that only a few were capable of singing properly. The words and melody to this particular Aria hadn't been heard in over ten thousand years.

The melody filled the room, the pure notes twisting inside and around each other, making an unearthly harmony.

The words of the song filled the Jackal with a level of fear and dread he'd never felt before. Of all the attacks he'd expected to face from his enemy, this was the one thing he could never have prepared for!

It was impossible! The boy was singing a song that the Jackal himself had written long ago, before he'd fallen from the Higher Places. It was a Song of Power that had been lost in the eons of time, that had not been known since the Jackal had gone by a different name and led the Guardian choirs. Images from that time filled the Jackal's consciousness; long forgotten memories of the time when he had been the highest, most beloved Guardian.

The words of the ancient song spoke of love, redemption, forgiveness, and restoration. They were powerful qualities the Jackal had abandoned when he fell, cursing such attributes as weakness. In his quest for power, he'd turned from that beauty and traded it for ashes and dust.

As the boy sang, the Jackal knew that his doom had come. In spite of everything he'd planned, the Bridge Builder had not been stopped. The boy was using what the Jackal had once been to defeat him, and there was nothing he could do to stand against it.

The Jackal's eye swiveled in its metal socket, rolling with fear. His metal valves hissed and the mechanical marvels that allowed him to hear and process the song ground to a screeching halt. The song was all around him now, and its power was far greater than any he'd ever faced.

Rusted bolts shot from his metal casings and steam burst from his broken valves. He tried to muster his dark power but found that he could not. The song was too strong!

A hissing scream escaped from his bellows and dread filled what remained of his tattered soul.

As the song continued to build, rays of light burst from Edward's fingertips, shooting directly into the heart of the black machinery. Edward could feel the power surging through his arms and fingers, a light tingle that made every nerve in his body feel wonderfully alive.

He knew with certainty that what he sang was more powerful than any of the Ten Words of Power, that this time using such powerful magic wouldn't deplete him.

The song redoubled in intensity, rising to a higher pitch. Edward could feel the power building around him, electrifying the air. The hairs on his arms and neck were standing on end. And as he sang, a tremendous joy filled his heart.

Edward felt love and compassion like he'd never known before. It was love without condition. He was filled with love for his parents and his loyal friends. But the song made him feel love that extended even to those who had intended him harm. He suddenly wished that they could understand, could step out of the darkness that blinded them and embrace what was good and true.

As Edward's song crescendoed, the Jackal's machine flew apart. Twisted metal and melted cogs shot in all directions. Edward was flung backward under the impact. As he fell, he wrapped his wings protectively around himself. He crashed to the ground as a shower of broken metal and rusted parts cascaded down around him.

As the last pieces clattered to the ground, Edward lifted his head from under his wing and gazed around at the wreckage. The pulsing walls that had seemed to be made of flesh were now ordinary stone. His eyes traveled to the corner of the room. Amid the rubble, a broken bellows collapsed with a soft wheezing sound.

It was the Jackal's dying breath.

Edward stood up and carefully examined all of the metal wreckage. He could find no trace of the yellow eye. Edward couldn't help wondering if the thing had gone to Specter's Hollow, and if it had, what unimaginable fears it might face when it got there.

✦　✦　✦

Outside, in the Jackal's throne room, rock and debris rained down upon the two armies. The Lair was falling apart! As their dark kingdom crumbled, the Groundlings shrieked and threw down their weapons. The crumbling Lair could only mean that their master's doom had come, and without his dark power to command them, most of the Groundlings lost whatever amount of courage they had possessed.

The few that resisted were dispatched. Joyce and Tabitha had trained their new recruits well! The rings hit their targets with unswerving accuracy.

Edward reentered the Jackal's throne room just in time to see Bridgette approach the writhing form of what had once been Whiplash Scruggs. When the beast saw what she carried, he let out a long, enraged howl. The girl lifted the silver shears to the crumpled, useless wings on his back and said, "It's time to face your fears and join your master, Moloc."

And with two quick snips, the terrible creature was gone.

Chapter Twenty-Three

MOTHER

With the Jackal destroyed, the impenetrable magic that surrounded Sarah Macleod's cage faded away and Edward's mother awoke from her long, enchanted sleep. She sat up in her cage and stared at the Guardians gathered around her.

Sarah noticed a majestic-looking Guardian nearby. He was crouched down over a small, crumpled body on the marble floor. The boy reminded her of someone. The Guardian stood and turned, and she saw who it was.

Tears sprang to Sarah's eyes as her son approached her gilded cage. Edward beamed at her, his face radiant with barely contained joy. He reached into his pocket and produced the magical key that Cornelius had given him. In his panic earlier, he had forgotten that he

had it. A lock materialized within the bars
and he inserted it.

With a small *click*, the bars swung open.

Edward took his mother's hand and helped
her out of the cage. Sarah looked up at her son,
taking in his dark hair and eyes, and marveling at
the huge wings that hung from his shoulders.

She held her hands to her mouth as grateful
tears cascaded down her cheeks. Every Guardian
and mortal who had come to Edward's aid stood
in awed silence as the Bridge Builder and the
Blue Lady stared into each other's eyes.

A smile like a dazzling sunrise played on
Edward's lips. Gripping his mother in a gentle
hug, he whispered, "Hi, Mom."

✦ Chapter Twenty-Four ✦
BRIDGES

At no time in the Woodbine's history had a bigger crowd assembled. Word had spread quickly of the Jackal's defeat. The news that the Bridge Builder had come and was going to repair the bridges between the worlds was on everyone's lips. Guardians and mortals stretched to the horizon, as far as the eye could see, waiting for Edward.

Edward allowed his mother to buckle the final strap on his new Guardian armor. It was made of white scales and shimmered in the afternoon sunlight.

"You look so much like your father," Sarah said.

Edward glanced over at her and smiled. She looked beautiful, dressed in a royal blue gown and wearing a silver circlet upon her head.

"I wish he were here with us," Edward said wistfully.

"Oh, but he is," said a second voice. Edward turned to see Jack the faun approaching. "Well, he's not far, anyway. Tollers got word from Specter's Hollow a few hours ago. Melchior passed through almost immediately. He's probably waiting for you in the Higher Places even as we speak."

Edward's heart pounded with excitement. After the bridges were rebuilt, they would truly be a family.

A Guardian with short, cropped hair and beautiful pink wings ran up to Edward. She gave his armor an appraising glance and nodded appreciatively.

"Now that's more like it! Much better than that old sweater!"

Edward beamed at her. "Thanks," he said. "By the way, how are the wings?"

Tabitha gave them an experimental flap. "Better than ever!" she exclaimed. "Thanks for leading the choir in that unusual Restoration Song of yours. Where did you learn it? You'll have to teach it to me sometime."

"I would if I could," Edward said with a smile. "But most of the time, I just sing whatever pops into my mind."

Suddenly the sound of a trumpet blast split the air.

"It's time!" Jack said with a grin. "Let's go show that Guardian Council something they'll never forget, eh?" He winked up at Edward.

Edward's stomach was full of butterflies. As he followed Jack, he noticed that Bridgette was nowhere to be seen. Concerned, he pulled Tabitha aside and whispered, "Have you seen Bridgette?"

The Guardian shook her head. "The last time I saw her was after we left the Jackal's fortress."

Edward continued to walk, growing more and more concerned. Where was she? Had something happened? His brown eyes scanned the crowd. There were mortals of all shapes, sizes, and appearances. He spotted the praying mantis in her flowing Chinese robes and the group of Swiss army horned unicorns who he'd seen at the Dancing Faun when he'd first arrived in the Woodbine. They waved at him and he returned the wave with a smile. Then, just as he approached the crest of a hill, he spotted her. She was standing off from the crowd, beneath a tall tree.

"Tell them to wait for me," he said to a protesting Tabitha as he elbowed through the crowd and ran over to Bridgette.

Jack stepped up to the podium and waved for the crowd's attention. They listened as he embarked on a long speech, detailing the history of the Woodbine and the prophetic arrival of the Bridge Builder. The faun had made certain that Zephath and the rest of the Guardian Council were given front row seats for this part of the event, and relished the humble expressions on their usually haughty faces.

Edward dashed up the hill to where Bridgette stood and was surprised to see that she'd been crying.

"Hi, Bridgette. What's the matter?" he asked, concerned.

The girl wiped her red, swollen eyes and said, "Once you rebuild the bridges, I w-won't be able to come with you."

Edward stared at her, confused. "Of course you will," he said gently. "Everybody who wants to leave the Woodbine can come."

She stared up at him with an anguished expression on her face. "You don't understand. It's not that I don't want to. I do. It's just that . . ." Her voice trailed off.

Edward put his arm around her and gave her a hug. "It's okay," he said reassuringly. "I'll be right beside you."

She gently took his arm from her shoulders. Turning from him, she said, "I can't go because I'm not able to. I'm in a coma back on Earth, remember? I'm trapped both here in the Woodbine and in the hospital. The doctors are treating my burns. I . . . If I try I can almost feel them working, even though I'm also here with you. They're trying to keep me alive, even though I might never wake up. I can't go with you if I'm still there."

Edward could see the pain on Bridgette's face. She was trapped between life and death. He thought back to the moment when she'd told him about the fire that had so severely burned her and had taken her baby sister's life. Then he thought of all the times that Bridgette had encouraged him, helping him press forward even though he didn't believe in himself. She had been there from the beginning, offering kindness and friendship at every turn. Without her help, Edward wouldn't be standing here now.

Turning her gently so he could look into her eyes, he tilted her tear-streaked face up toward his own.

"Bridgette, no matter what happens, even if I rebuild the bridge and everybody in the Woodbine goes forward, I'm not going to leave you behind."

Bridgette rushed into Edward's arms. The two held each other for a long time, not saying anything. Finally Bridgette stepped back, her eyes still shining with tears. She gave Edward a watery smile and said, "Well, it sounds like the crowd has heard just about enough of Jack's speech. I think it's time for you to do some bridge building."

Edward smiled down at her. He took her

small hand in his own and the two of them walked down the hill to the podium where Jack stood, wrapping up his long speech.

As Edward and Bridgette approached, a cheer erupted from the crowd. Edward felt a renewed sense of nerves as he surveyed the huge pieces of stone scattered all around the destroyed fortress. They were the remains of the first bridge—huge, oblong pieces of stone that weighed several thousand tons each.

Edward hadn't formed a plan for building the bridges. He'd assumed, like the other times, that when the moment came he would just know what to do. But now, as the crowd fell into a hushed silence, he found that he didn't have the slightest idea how to proceed.

Edward stared at the field, thousands of eyes boring into him. Here he was, the supposed Bridge Builder, and he had no idea how to do it! His heart started racing and he licked his dry lips. Murmurs spread through the concerned assembly. Everyone wondered what Edward was waiting for.

Edward's hand flicked down to his pocket.

It was an old habit of his, reaching for his deck of playing cards whenever he felt nervous. He wished he had his cards now. It had been so long since he'd felt their reassuring touch.

Edward had purged the poison of the Four from his system when he sang his Song of Power, but there was still a voice in his head. This time it was his own, wondering if he was the prophetic hero after all. Maybe it had all been a gigantic coincidence. What did he know about building bridges? The only thing he'd ever been able to build was card houses . . .

That was when it hit him.

As Edward gazed at the huge, oblong pieces of stone, a huge smile spread across his face. There they were, scattered among the ruins. Fifty-four of the most perfectly shaped pieces of stone he could imagine.

He knew what to do.

One by one the images of his long lost deck flashed through his mind. He visualized placing the cards against one another, as he'd done when building his countless card houses, and a song burst from his lips, a triumphant song the likes of which had never been heard in any of the Seven Worlds.

It was in a new language, and as he sang, the huge pieces of stone broke free from where they'd been sitting for thousands of years. Centuries of earth trailed from their flattened edges as they followed the ornate pattern that Edward created. One by one, the pieces settled upon each other, eliciting gasps from the awestruck crowd. The mammoth stones stretched an infinite distance, soaring up toward the worlds beyond.

Edward knew that it was but one of the Seven Bridges that he was rebuilding. There were four more that needed his attention, and to get to them he would have to travel upward and find the waiting pieces.

Once more the opening lines of the prophetic rhyme echoed in his mind.

There are seven bridges between the worlds
And five of them are broken.
The sixth one has no rails to hold
And the seventh one was stolen.

He didn't know about the sixth and seventh bridges. From the sound of the verses, it seemed that the sixth must be intact but hard to cross. As far as the seventh one went, he could only wonder who had stolen it and why? If there were no pieces, he would have to find another way to build the bridge.

The last stone rose into the air, soaring upward until it was lost in the clouds, journeying to take its place at the end of the long line of others. Nobody but Edward could see where it was supposed to fit, but in his mind Edward saw the last piece of the puzzle perfectly. And with a satisfying *click* it fell into place.

The fully restored bridge shimmered with a gentle light. The awestruck crowd finally found their voices. A mighty cheer resonated through the Woodbine, making the ground shake.

It had happened. The first of the five bridges that the Jackal had broken was rebuilt. The countless souls trapped in the Woodbine for thousands of years would finally be able to journey upward.

Edward's mother stood beside him, a look

of fierce pride written on her face. Edward wondered if his father could somehow see him, or if he knew what Edward had done.

His thoughts were interrupted by the Guardian High Council, who sheepishly congratulated him and suggested that Jack should be the first to set foot on the newly made bridge. Jack hesitated, insisting that Edward take the historic step. But Edward was thinking about Bridgette and told Jack that he should do it. After all, it was Jack who had recognized Edward for who he truly was.

Jack nodded and, extending his hand to Joyce, led the procession of souls to Lelakek, the world that legends said was closest to the Woodbine.

Edward stood, his hand clasped in Bridgette's, watching as the steady stream of Woodbine inhabitants made their way up the bridge.

Tabitha, Rachel, and the other young Guardians who had participated in the battle had decided to see what lay beyond, and they had invited Melchior's old friends Sariel and Artemis to go with them. Edward noticed that for once the two creatures weren't fighting with each other, but wore huge smiles, glad to be included once more among the ranks of their Guardian peers. Although they had fallen, they had earned their redemption at last. Edward knew that he never would have succeeded without the help they had offered both him and his father.

As the sun sank lower in the sky, the crowd of people started to thin. Edward watched as two of Cornelius's big, blue snails slowly advanced up the bridge, following the last of the stragglers.

Neither Edward nor Bridgette spoke as the last few people ascended the bridge. Some of them shot curious glances back at Edward, wondering why the Bridge Builder himself wasn't going with them. Edward smiled and waved, insisting that they go on without him.

The sky turned crimson as the sun set behind the mountains. Edward didn't look, but he could tell Bridgette had started to cry. *Faith, faith. Have faith . . .*

He repeated the words over and over again in his mind. Too many times before, when all hope was gone and everything seemed lost, he had given up. If he hadn't learned by now to have faith, then he'd learned nothing at all.

Just as he was about to ask his mother to go
on without him, there was the sound of small
footsteps running up behind him. Edward
turned and saw Tollers, red-faced and puffing,
coming up the hill.

"It's all right! It's all right!" he wheezed as he
approached. Edward looked at him, confused.

"What's all right?" he asked.

Tollers pointed his tiny finger at Bridgette.
"Word . . . just came . . . from Earth," he said,
his voice punctuated by gasps. "Bridgette's been
released! She's now an official resident."

Bridgette felt something the moment Tollers
said the words. It was as if heavy chains deep
inside her had fallen away, leaving her with a new
sense of freedom. She felt more alive, more *real*
than she'd ever been.

She looked up at Edward, too stunned to
speak. He gazed down at her, his eyes twinkling
with happiness. Then, with a whoop of joy,
Edward gathered her into his arms.

✦ ✦ ✦

Silhouetted against a sea of glittering stars, Edward, Bridgette, and Sarah approached the bridge. Edward spread his long, ebony wings, stretching them protectively around the people he loved most in the world. As his feet touched the bridge and he began his long walk to the heavens, he felt joy like he'd never known before. Edward knew there was still work to be done, but for now he was at peace.

The Bridge Builder began to sing.

✦ Appendix ✦

Beezlenut's Guide to the Afterlife

The following is an updated excerpt from
Beezlenut's Guide to the Afterlife regarding the worlds
between Earth and the Higher Places. This is the
most current information available to travelers
since the arrival of the Bridge Builder, and is
changing as new discoveries filter back from
Guardian Scouts.

The Woodbine

Designed as a brief stopping place, the
Woodbine is a place where souls can take care
of unfinished business on Earth. From the
Woodbine, a mortal is free to request that a
Guardian be sent to provide comfort or healing
to loved ones left behind.

Occasionally, a mortal wishes to communicate
a message to their loved ones. This is more
complicated, as Guardians are invisible to
mortals and cannot communicate with them
directly. Guardians *are* visible to animals, and

often use pets to help a loved one find something or to provide extra comfort.

For thousands of years, mortals were stuck in the Woodbine, unable to move on even after their business on Earth was completed. However, with the reconstruction of the bridge, they are now free to travel upward when they feel ready to do so.

Lelakek

Lelakek's reputation for having a perfect climate and majestic mountains has circulated throughout the Woodbine for centuries. In fact, the Afterlife's second world is so beautiful that many mortals have stopped on their journey upward to become permanent residents. When interviewed, most explained that their reason for stopping was because they believed that the Higher Places couldn't be any more gorgeous.

But Lelakek has more than gorgeous scenery. It is home to a species of bird so rare and beautiful that it caused endless arguments over what to name it. Consequently, the bird has been labeled the "No-Name Thrush." The bird is covered with plumage that has a mirrorlike sheen and reflects the colors around it. It also has a magnificent crown of thin, wiry feathers on its head that vibrate like harp strings and produce a single, beautiful note that adds harmony to its distinctive song.

Travelers should be sure to keep an eye out for this unique bird.

Although Lelakek's beauty is sure to draw visitors, the real highlight here—and the reason for this world's stellar reputation—are the unforgettable feasts prepared by Guardian chefs. One restaurant worth visiting is The Broken Wing, run by Chef Jean-Paul Ange, which received the prestigious Five Rings award from *Bridges Restaurant Quarterly*.

It is said that Jean-Paul's chefs, nicknamed "tabach" in the Guardian tongue, undergo many years of training before they're allowed to cook their first dish. The training is kept very secret, but rumors abound about strange and bizarre rituals that require the ultimate in physical skill and mental concentration.

A recent report from an anonymous tabach

described a training ritual that involves gathering fire berries from a bush that can only be found in the molten core of Lelakek. The chef-in-training must tunnel beneath the ground for miles before diving into the core's flames and retrieving the berries.

Considering that "flame berry" tea cake is one of the simplest and most common recipes on Lelakek, one can only speculate what kind of training creating a savory dish like Roast Griffin Framboise would require!

The guide heartily suggests that visitors to this spectacular world come hungry!

Jubal

Built millennia ago by famous Guardian Josiah Goodwin, the legendary Ten Thousand Mile Maze is a "must do" experience for any visitor to Jubal. In fact, the only way for a visitor to ascend to the next world is to complete the labyrinth.

The maze's beautiful stone arch entrance is well-known for the blue sage that grows on it. As most Woodbine botanists know, blue sage is famous for being a "philosopher plant," one of the few plant species that can actually speak. Upon entry to the maze, each walker is treated to a spiritual question posed by the sage plant. The walker is then left to ponder the question while he or she wanders the endless, twisting paths. Questions range from abstract queries like, "Do I know when I've had enough?" to somewhat comical questions such as, "What is the meaning of fish and why are there so many of them in the sea?"

The maze's interior is constructed out of so many different materials that the terrain changes every few steps. A typical visit may begin on a pathway of ornately decorated stones and suddenly wind into a majestic crystal forest. Walkers have also reported twisting paths built high on stilts that stretch over an endless horizon of glittering, crimson seas.

Fortunately, rest areas are in abundance throughout all parts of the labyrinth. These areas are constantly supplied with food and drink, and provide a wonderful opportunity to rest or interact with other walkers.

Jubal has been rated by *Afterlife 100* magazine as the third-best stopping place for those travelers wishing to probe the deeper meanings of life or wanting a really good nap somewhere extraordinary.

Baradil

Perpetually shrouded in fog, Baradil remains one of the most mysterious and unexplored worlds of the Afterlife. The few reports that have come back tell of a place so dense with clouds that very few details about the terrain can be made out.

Baradil is said to be a place where one can discover "self awareness," but because there are so few reports, this cannot be confirmed. Further updates from the guide will be provided when available.

Akamai

The legendary Akamai is known for its extensive music library, which houses every Guardian song ever written. The library is a tremendous resource for Guardians interested in composing Songs of Power and a wonderful place for mortal travelers to witness firsthand the magic of newly invented songs. It is also the place where mortals and Guardians research songs to help them build vehicles to cross the bridge without rails on Zeshar.

The traveler to Akamai should be aware that the lands outside the library are filled with dangerous creatures. The library is well guarded, with sentries posted along its castlelike walls. Since it is the only habitable structure on this world, travelers are advised to stay inside the library building at all times. The structure is expansive, with sleeping quarters and several very nice restaurants housed within, so visitors need not worry about comfortable accommodations.

Scattered throughout the library's huge rooms are several viewing areas constructed on high platforms. And unlike most libraries, loud noises are encouraged here! Because thousands of compositions are being sung or played on Instruments of Power all at once, the noise can be somewhat overwhelming at first. But most travelers report being able to make sense of the chaos after spending an hour or so listening to the individual melodies.

For best viewing, it is suggested that visitors remain in the library after dark. The magical properties of the songs glow with resplendent color at that time and can be quite spectacular. Equally entertaining are the songs that don't turn out quite right, such as the famous "Song of Wondrous Fruit" that ended up showering everyone inside the library with green pomegranate juice.

Several new Songs of Power have been composed since the rediscovery of Akamai. Among these are "Jezreel's Song of Battle," which produced glowing spears over fifty yards long, and "Lissa's Lament," which created a steady rain of sweets (much to the delight of the younger mortal travelers).

Zeshar

A favorite of mechanical-minded people everywhere, Zeshar is a wonderful place to visit for anyone who loves invention and clever machines. The famous pastime on this world is the construction of vehicles to cross the famous "Sixth Bridge" that has no rails. Each vehicle is unique, and any mortal or Guardian wishing to cross must invent his or her own, using the Song of Power written or found while visiting Akamai.

Zeshar is a hot, arid world. Luckily, numerous magically cooled tents have been constructed next to the "Giant's Raceway," the nickname for the bridge that connects Zeshar to Iona. When visiting Zeshar, it is recommended that tourists learn a few of the local expressions. A visitor watching the various vehicles that attempt to cross the bridge might be confused when a local shouts out, "Cross that crazy freen-burn, you slobby shorker!" (Translation: "Freen-burn" is a nice, wide racetrack and "slobby shorker" is a gifted mechanic with no talent for driving.*)

The races across the bridge are exciting and filled with suspense, however travelers are advised to carry ear protection due to the tremendous roar of the engines.

*An excellent resource on local dialects can be found in the second edition of *Beezlenut's Guide to Afterlife Slang*, published in W.R. 1270.

Vehicles that don't make it across the bridge, or accidentally drive off the side, are rescued by specially trained Guardians. This troop of exceptionally strong Guardians is trained to catch vehicles that plunge over the edge of the bridge or tow vehicles with a malfunction back to the starting line.

Surprisingly, there have been very few major accidents in Zeshar's history.

No trip to Zeshar would be complete without a visit to Farley's Garage, a museum built by a mortal named Farley Farnsworth that houses some of the more spectacular vehicles invented throughout Zeshar's history. This includes the "Feathered Funicula," an incredible flying chair that traversed the bridge at record speeds, and the "Washburn Wonder," a vehicle with so many wheels that they almost stretch the length of the bridge itself!

Drivers that make it across the bridge in record time have a special honor bestowed upon them. Their names, along with drawings of their vehicles, are inscribed in the prestigious *Farnsworth's Book of Speed Records*.

The Blown Engine, a small, inexpensive diner, is attached to Farley's Garage for those budget-conscious travelers who want a simple meal at a fair price.

Iona

To date, Iona has remained largely unexplored. This is partly due to most people's desire to travel through it and get to the Higher Places as quickly as possible. However, visitors have also reported finding the terrible storms and freezing, iodine seas unpleasant.

The last of the worlds between Earth and the Higher Places has come under much scrutiny of late. As most travelers know, the bridge between Iona and the Higher Places was stolen by the Jackal in W.R. 60. Rumors exist of a replacement bridge that only those whose hearts are pure can see. However, there has been no confirmation of these rumors. Thankfully, a clever group of Guardians have designed majestic ships to ferry visitors from the docks of Iona to the shores of the Higher Places. These boats serve as the primary source of transportation across the water, and will likely remain so until a new bridge can be built or the location of the original found.

Unfortunately, the Afterlife Emporium offices have recently received unsettling reports of the famous ships disappearing with entire groups of passengers aboard. The Guardian Council is investigating the matter and suspects Groundling activity. Whether or not the Jackal's influence is still felt on this remote world remains to be seen.

If you enjoyed *The Mysterious Mr. Spines*,
be sure to check out

The Misadventures of
Benjamin Bartholomew Piff

*B*enjamin Bartholomew Piff scraped out the remains of last week's dinner—a hideous, soupy concoction of clams, spinach, and leftover meatloaf—from inside the immense iron pot. He tried not to retch as he attacked the moldy remains, armed only with a toothbrush. The punishment had been forced upon him by the orphanage chef, who Ben feared and hated more than anyone else: a horrible and greasy old man named Solomon Roach.

"MR. PIFF!" The crusty chef's irritated voice echoed from somewhere above him. Ben stood, his knees dripping with grease and grime, to peer up over the edge of the giant pot.

"Yes, Mr. Roach?"

"When you finish that pot, I have four more that need scrubbing." The gangly cook's black marblelike eyes bore into Ben, a twisted leer curling his upper lip. "I want them all finished by ten o'clock, got it?"

"Yeah, okay."

"What?" Roach's eyes narrowed. "I didn't hear that."

"Yes, Mr. Roach."

Feeling satisfied, the cook grunted his approval and stomped from the room, banging the rusted kitchen door behind him.

Ben looked over to the four humongous remaining pots. *And all because I said I didn't want seconds,* Ben thought miserably. Breakfast had consisted of Mr. Roach's usual inedible fare. This morning it was grayish oatmeal topped with boiled beets, and Ben had felt like if he had taken Roach's offer for seconds, he would have thrown up. The consequences for not wanting to eat more of the cook's latest creation was to report to the kitchen and endure three hours of scrubbing, a punishment that was meant to make him a "more grateful and well-mannered boy."

He sighed as he resumed cleaning. It seemed like Mr. Roach was always looking for opportunities to punish him, whether he had done anything wrong or not.

Well, that's all going to change after tonight. Ben grinned as he finished scrubbing the first pot and climbed into the second. He had plotted his escape for weeks, and tonight was the big night. If his plan worked, he would never have to set foot within a thousand miles of a stew pot for the rest of his life.

He finally finished the gruesome job at two minutes to ten, and, without waiting for Mr. Roach to come in and check on his handiwork, he hastily returned the worn toothbrush to the chipped ceramic holder mounted on the wall next to the giant pots. Then, opening an unused bottom drawer inside one of the kitchen cabinets, he removed a small bundled bag that he had hidden earlier.

Ben dashed out the back door of the kitchen and raced through the grass of the backyard to his secret hiding spot.

"Hi, Rags," Benjamin greeted the happy terrier as he crawled into the oversize doghouse. He turned the lock he had installed on the doghouse door and, with a small *thud,* set the tightly wrapped bundle on the dirt floor next to the shaggy pup.

As he peered around the inside of the doghouse, Ben allowed himself a small secret smile. His drawings decorated the walls, and a plain, ragged pillow that he had secreted away from his shabby bedroom served as a seat. He plopped down upon it and opened the small package.

Ever since the tragic accident the year before—the airplane crash that had taken his parents away—Benjamin had lived at Pinch's Home for Wayward Boys, a dilapidated orphanage converted from a windowless industrial building that once produced dental tools. Ben hated the place and had good reasons for thinking that it was a joke that it even had the word "home" in its title, for there was nothing about it that felt welcoming at all.

First of all, there was the boys' sleeping quarters. Ben spent his nights in a damp cinder-block room that looked much more like a prison cell than a bedroom, and was filled end to end with rusted army cots. All of the boys at the orphanage slept in the overcrowded room, and there was hardly any space to walk without banging a knee on a piece of furniture or tripping over a pair of shoes that had been left by the edge of someone's cot. It was hot and humid in the summer and ice cold in the winter, and Ben wasn't allowed to hang even a single picture on any of the walls.

Secondly, there was the smell of the place. When Ben first arrived, the overpowering stench of pine-scented ammonia had assaulted him. He had felt dizzy for days because of the poorly ventilated hallways. He soon discovered that the pine smell masked a much darker, more sinister odor, something like a mountain of mildewed socks that hadn't been washed in months, and which seemed to emanate from some secret place in the building's basement.

Lastly, and most importantly, there were the two people that looked for ways to make his life in the bleak institution as difficult as possible. The first was the head of the orphanage, Ms. Eliza Pinch, a tall, skinny, elderly spinster whose perfume smelled of an old cat box. Why she had ever opened an orphanage was unfathomable to Ben, for she was very vocal about her hatred for children and seemed to harbor a special loathing just for him.

Mr. Roach was the self-appointed "Discipline Master" at the orphanage, and loved nothing more than to dish out punishments to any orphan who looked at him the wrong way. Ben had spent many terrible nights scrubbing the smelly kitchen under Roach's watchful eye, and deeply resented being punished for imagined crimes that he hadn't committed.

Life was certainly a lot different for him now than it had been a year earlier. He'd had a room of his own with a breathtaking view of the mountains, a big television set that could play DVDs and video games . . . and two wonderful parents who loved him more than anything.

Ben would give anything in the whole world to have his parents back for just one day.

Looking down, he opened the bundle and examined what he had smuggled into the doghouse. Twenty dollars in quarters, his savings from helping out Mr. Kunkel, the kindly gardener who had been fired two weeks ago, was shoved inside an old tube sock.

Ms. Pinch regularly searched Ben's possessions, which were kept in an old shoebox underneath his cot. The old woman insisted that the reason for this was simply "routine inspection," but she inspected Ben's box twice as often as the other boys', and Ben suspected that she was hoping to find something that would get him into trouble. Ben had learned from experience that it was in his best interest to hide whatever small valuables he had, or they would mysteriously disappear while being subjected to one of Ms. Pinch's probing searches.

After carefully placing a rusty pocketknife with a broken blade on the ground next to his concealed money, he reached inside the bag and produced his meager food stores. Next to the knife and sock, he set a tin of Vienna sausages and a small foil-wrapped package of frosted Pop-Tarts, both of which he had liberated from the school kitchen two weeks ago during a punishment from Mr. Roach.

He would kill me if he knew. The thought of the greasy cook finding out that he had taken the food filled Ben with dread.

He had a fleeting memory of his first week at the orphanage, when, assuming that he was allowed to eat like he had at home, he had taken a cookie from the chipped jar on the cafeteria counter. The other boys in line had let out a collective gasp when they saw what he had done, and it had taken little time for Ben to realize why they'd reacted with such alarm.

To his surprise and horror, Ben found himself dragged by his ear into the orphanage's filthy kitchen and was roughly forced to climb inside and scrub out Roach's giant blackened stew vats. He soon found out that it was only the first of what would turn out to be daily visits to the horrible place.

Later that night, one of the littlest boys at the orphanage, a five-year-old named Shane, brought Ben a small piece of leftover bread that he had saved from his own meal. It was thoughtful, since Ben hadn't been allowed to eat dinner, but his appetite had completely disappeared after spending so much time inside the reeking filth of Roach's pots.

It didn't take long after that first awful week for Ben's thoughts to turn toward planning an escape.

Now, if he could just make it to the bus station tonight without anybody noticing, he would be home free.

He reached into the bag and pulled out the last of his treasures. A small cardboard frame held a photo of a smiling man and woman at the beach. Ben was perched upon his father's shoulders and was grinning happily, his hand raised and holding a gleaming white sand dollar.

He gazed wistfully at the photo, recalling the happy day.

His throat tightening with emotion, he placed the photo back in the bag and gathered up his other things. Rags moved over to the bag and sniffed it curiously.

"Not yet. You can have some sausages when we leave tonight." Ben scratched the hungry puppy behind the ears.

Rags had technically been Mr. Kunkel's dog (the rules at the orphanage were clear about the students not having any pets), but Mr. Kunkel had allowed Ben to secretly care for the puppy, a stray that had wandered onto the school grounds. Rags was Ben's best friend, and, now that Mr. Kunkel was gone, they were together whenever possible. Ben sneaked into the forbidden doghouse for comfort, when he could manage it.

Suddenly the sound of a car engine caught Ben's attention. He peered through the cracked wood of the doghouse at a black Oldsmobile that had pulled through the rusty gates and watched as the car wound its way up the cracked cement driveway to the main entrance of the orphanage.

"Ms. Bloom," he whispered. *I wonder what she's doing here?*

Ben hadn't seen the prim, well-dressed social worker since he had first been admitted to the orphanage. She carried a small package in her arms and, opening the bent screen door, knocked crisply.

A moment later, the lean, hawklike form of Ms. Pinch appeared in the doorway. Ben couldn't make out what was said, but he saw Ms. Pinch nod sourly, then motion vaguely toward the backyard.

I gotta get out of here, Ben thought, glancing around desperately.

He had barely squeezed out of the doghouse door when he heard the raspy shout.

"BENJAMIN PIFF!"